W9-BUG-328

THE SHERLOCK FILES

CASES: UNSOLVED

BOOK 4

THE

◆ MISSING HEIR ◆

THE SHERLOCK FILES

CASES: UNSOLVED

BOOK 4

THE
◆ MISSING HEIR ◆

TRACY BARRETT

Henry Holt and Company
New York

Henry Holt and Company, LLC
Publishers since 1866
175 Fifth Avenue
New York, New York 10010
mackids.com

Henry Holt® is a registered trademark of Henry Holt and Company, LLC.

Library of Congress Cataloging-in-Publication Data
Barrett, Tracy.
The missing heir / by Tracy Barrett.—1st ed.
p. cm. — (The Sherlock files ; 4)
Summary: Xena and Xander Holmes, an American brother and sister living
in London, use clues from their ancestor Sherlock Holmes' casebook to help
classmate Alice Banders, who goes missing following the announcement
that she will be crowned queen of Borogovia after her thirteenth birthday.
ISBN 978-0-8050-8047-6
[1. Mystery and detective stories. 2. Missing persons—Fiction.
3. Princesses—Fiction. 4. Identity—Fiction. 5. Brothers and sisters—
Fiction. 6. London (England)—Fiction. 7. England—Fiction.] I. Title.
PZ7.B275355Mis 2011 [Fic]—dc22 2010041012

First Edition—2011
Book designed by Greg Wozney/Illustrated by Richard Carbajal
Printed in May 2011 in the United States of America by R. R. Donnelly &
Sons Company, Har

10 9 8 7 6 5 4 3

but hadn't solved. Xander flipped past the three cold cases that he and Xena had already solved and found the pages where Borogovia was mentioned. A newspaper clipping was tucked into the notebook too. Xena tried not to show her impatience while Xander read the pages more quickly than she ever could.

"Wow, this is pretty amazing!" Xander finally said. "There was this princess of Borogovia who got kidnapped."

"What happened?" Xena asked.

"She was just a baby, it says here in the newspaper. Her parents were away because her mom, Queen Charlotte, got sick after the baby was born, so her husband, King Boris, took her on a cruise." Xander picked up another clipping and frowned. "Huh!"

"What?" Xander was so annoying sometimes.

"The baby was returned a few weeks later, right before the king and queen got home. She wasn't hurt or anything. So I wonder why they called Sherlock in."

"Maybe Alice knows something about it," Xena said. "I'll ask Mom if we can stay after school tomorrow. Then we can get more information from her."

The Borogovia Jou

Sunday, December 16, 1894

PRINCESS STELLA KIDNAPPED!

The happy Queen Charlotte and King Boris holding the new baby Princess just days after her birth.

By Christopher Harris

Princess Stella of Borogovia was found missing the morning of December 13. The Princess, daughter of Queen Charlotte and King Boris, was only a few weeks old. The King and Queen were away on a cruise when the baby was kidnapped. King Boris planned the trip when Queen Charlotte became ill shortly after giving birth.

Members of the royal staff, including the parlor maids, the gardeners, and the new nanny Miss Eugenia Mimsy are being questioned.

Continued on page 3

DEC

By Nath

Despi
on th
said
abou
cont
sti
cal
inv
wor
He
but
thin
cou

If
fir
he
Alt
for
rema

The Borogovia Jou

Wednesday, January 2, 1895

Missing Borogovian Princess Found

By Christopher Harris

Princess Stella, daughter of Queen Charlotte and King Boris, was returned safely to her home at the Borogovian Mansion Sunday morning. The Princess was kidnapped from her home a few weeks ago while her parents were on holiday. Authorities have not discovered the kidnapper's identity, and the royal family has hired Detective Sherlock Holmes to continue the investigation.

Continued on page 3

• • •

The next afternoon, at the end of the school day, the music teacher came on the intercom to remind everyone about the audition for a solo in the glee club recital the next week. The girl who was supposed to sing the soprano solo had gotten appendicitis and wouldn't be able to perform.

"I wonder if that's why Alice is staying late today," Xander said as he and Xena made their way down the corridor. "Is she a singer?"

"She said she wanted to be one," Xena said, "but I never heard her sing. I wonder if she's any good. That glee club concert will probably be right before she leaves to be crowned." It was still an odd thought, that timid Alice was about to become a queen.

Through the big windows that faced the street, Xena and Xander noticed a black limousine with windows tinted such a dark shade there was no way you could see inside it. It must be Alice's, Xena thought. A lot of their classmates had parents who were politicians and diplomats, but they had never seen this car before Alice had been revealed to be a princess. A group of photographers and reporters were hanging around it, looking hopefully at the school, and exhaust was coming out of the car, so Xena decided that Alice must still be inside the building.

"Isn't that her bodyguard?" Xander pointed down the hall. Xena caught sight of the man named Jasper standing near the auditorium door. She and Xander managed to make their way through the crowd of departing students, teachers giving instructions, and parents calling for their children, to where Alice was waiting in line for her turn to audition.

Alice gave Xena a shy smile. "Thanks for meeting me," she said. "We can give you a ride home afterward."

"Cool!" Xander said, but Xena dug him in the ribs. Their mother would kill them if they took a ride from someone she didn't know, even if it was a schoolmate.

"Thanks, but we'll take the Tube," Xena said. "So tell me about those letters that you found. We know there was a princess who was kidnapped around a hundred years ago, when you said they were written. Do the letters have anything to do with that?"

Alice dropped her voice and looked around, but everyone was too excited about spring break to pay them much attention. "Princess Stella, the kidnapped baby, was my great-great-grandmother. She was born here, in the same house where I live with my aunt Penelope."

"Why would a Borogovian princess be born in London?" Xander asked.

The girl in line in front of Alice was called, and she stepped into the auditorium. Alice's turn would be next.

"The princess's mother, Queen Charlotte, was English," Alice explained. "She wanted to have her baby here, where her own mother could be with her. Charlotte's own nanny had retired, and the queen was lonely in Borogovia, so she came here to be with her mom and to hire a new nanny. Anyway, the queen wrote those letters I found to a friend back in Borogovia. She wrote them after the baby had been kidnapped and returned."

"What did they say?" Xander was impatient. Any minute now, Alice would be called.

"I'm not exactly sure," she said. "I told Xena that the language is old-fashioned, and my formal Borogovian isn't very good—it's really different from the way people speak nowadays. But one of them seemed to say—"

"Alice Banders!" the music teacher called from inside the auditorium.

"Wait!" Xander stepped between Alice and the door. She hesitated, looking from him to Xena and back again. "Can't you at least tell us what the letters are about?"

"Alice Banders!" came from the auditorium again, this time with an edge of impatience to it.

The girl behind Alice said, "Come *on*! If you don't want to do it, just say so. My mother's waiting."

"It's too complicated," Alice said to Xena. "I can't just . . ." Her voice trailed off as she pushed past Xander and disappeared into the large room.

CHAPTER THREE

After a minute, Xena slipped into the auditorium. She stood in the shadows at the edge of the large room as Alice walked onto the stage. Xena didn't think she would have recognized her if she hadn't known that Alice was going to be the next one to audition. Alice took long, confident strides and lifted her chin, a faint smile on her lips. The bright stage lights made her blond hair almost sparkle.

"Is that really *Alice?*" Xander had come in without Xena realizing it. "She looks so different!"

"Hush," Xena said as the music teacher, Ms. Shaw, said to Alice, "You may begin."

"I'll be singing 'Borogovia, My Home,'" Alice said. "It's the national anthem."

As the first note left her throat, Xena and Xander turned to each other, amazed. How could such a small, shy girl sing like that? They couldn't understand the words, but there was such love and longing in the music and in Alice's rich, sweet voice that the meaning was clear.

There was silence for a few moments after Alice came to the end. Then Miss Shaw cleared her throat and said, "You have the solo, my dear. And why haven't you been singing in the glee club all year?"

Suddenly Alice looked like the girl they knew. She seemed to shrink, and she hung her head. She mumbled something about not having enough time for extracurricular activities, but now that she was about to leave . . . then her voice trailed off.

Xena and Xander were back in the corridor when Alice came out, her face shining. Jasper hovered nearby, making it impossible to have a real conversation.

"Congratulations!" Xander said. "That was great!"

"Do you really think so?" Alice asked. They both nodded enthusiastically. "Oh good! I hope I sing well on the audition video for *Talented Brits*."

"You have to make a video?" Xena asked.

"I have to send them one by the middle of

next week," Alice said. "I don't know how to
it, but I have to figure it out. If it's good and they
choose me for a live audition, maybe my aunt
will change her mind and let me go." She didn't
sound very hopeful.

"Our mom has a new kind of video recorder
that supposedly has really good audio," Xander
said. "We can make it for you!"

"But school is out for a week," Xena said,
"so we can't do it here. Give me your cell number, and I'll call you so we can figure out a time
to do the recording."

"I don't have a cell phone anymore," Alice
said. "My aunt said I was spending too much
time texting my friends in Borogovia. You could
call me at my house, but calls are monitored for
security reasons."

"Why don't you come to our house over the
weekend?" Xander suggested.

The light that had come into Alice's eyes
during her audition dimmed and went out. "It's
hard. I have to have a bodyguard with me at all
times. But in my house the security is really
good, so we would be left alone. Do you want to
come over tomorrow?"

"Your Highness." They all jumped. They had

forgotten about Jasper. "You know that your aunt doesn't like to be kept waiting."

"Coming!" Alice quickly scribbled her address on a slip of paper that she passed to Xander. "Why don't you come early in the afternoon? I should be done with my work by then. And please—don't tell anybody about this."

Before they could ask Alice what kind of work she could possibly have on the first Saturday of spring break, Jasper took her firmly by the arm and led her out.

Xena and Xander had just stepped outside when their friend Andrew Watson, a fellow member of the Society for the Preservation of Famous Detectives, or SPFD, came up to them. He had been present when the SPFD, a group devoted to preserving the memories of great detectives from the past, had given Xena and Xander the cold-case notebook of their ancestor, Sherlock Holmes. At first Andrew hadn't been friendly with them—he had resented the attention Sherlock had gotten compared to his own great-great-great-grandfather, Sherlock's best friend, Dr. Watson. But Andrew had gotten over that, and he had been a great help in solving some of their earlier cases.

Andrew said, "Some of us from my class are going to celebrate the start of spring break at the bakery. Want to come along?"

Xander's stomach rumbled. He loved English food, and lately he had fallen for the muffins at the bakery near school. But he shook his head. "Got to get home."

"Suit yourself!" Andrew ran off and joined the others. Xander looked after them wistfully.

"It's okay," Xena said, knowing her brother wished he could have gone with them. "We have to make some sacrifices if we want to solve Sherlock's cold cases." Xander nodded without answering and followed her down the steps to the Tube.

Once home, while Xander fetched the casebook, Xena went online to find out more about the disappearance of Princess Stella more than a hundred years ago. Xena soon found a history of Borogovia written by a well-known scholar.

"Listen to this," she said when Xander came back with the worn leather-bound book. "In those days, when someone was sick, the doctors told them that sea air would make them better, so after the princess was born, King Boris and Queen Charlotte went to the Mediterranean—

you know, the sea around Italy and Greece?"

Xander nodded impatiently. He was good with factual subjects like geography—a photographic memory really came in handy for details.

"Anyway," Xena went on, "they left their baby in the Borogovian mansion with the new nanny, Miss Mimsy. So a week after they left, Miss Mimsy didn't come down to breakfast. One of the servants went to her room to see what was up. It says here"—she scanned the page and then read aloud—" 'The maid woke Miss Mimsy only with great difficulty, because, as it turned out, she had been drugged. A later analysis of the nanny's bedtime cocoa revealed the presence of an opiate.' " Xena looked at Xander. "What's that?"

"It's a kind of drug that makes you sleepy. What else does it say?"

"They noticed that the baby was missing. They searched all over and asked everyone, but no one had come in and taken her. The maid ran to the corner to get a policeman, and Miss Mimsy went to the telegraph office to send word to the king and queen."

"So they came right back?"

Xena scrolled down the page and shook her head. "Not for a few weeks. They couldn't get telegrams on the ship, and when they arrived at the next port, the telegram had been sent to the wrong address or something, and they never got it."

"That's so weird," Xander said. "I mean, remember when we were in that park with Mom and she took pictures of us and sent them to Aunt Lou? And she lives thousands of miles away, across the ocean!"

"I remember," Xena said, rolling her eyes. "She called Mom right away and Mom put her on speakerphone and everybody around us in the park got to hear how cute we were."

"And how she never would have recognized me," Xander added. "And it hasn't even been a year since we saw her!"

"Well, a cell phone would have been a help to King Boris and Queen Charlotte," Xena said. "After the telegram missed them, they were on the ship for a while and they didn't know anything about the kidnapping until they got to the next port, which was"—she paused and scanned the page again—"Naples, Italy. They read an English newspaper there that had an article about the princess, and they turned right around and came back. They'd been gone for almost a month. But then—and this is the strange part—the day before they got home, the baby was returned!"

"That's *weird*," Xander said. "You don't just borrow a baby!"

"I know. There was never a ransom note or any kind of threat, like, you know, *do something or I'll never return the princess*."

"What I don't get," Xander said, "is why they called in Sherlock. If the baby was back, what was he supposed to investigate? And if there wasn't a baby to be found, why is it in his cold-case notebook? That's supposed to be just for cases he didn't solve."

"I guess they wanted to find out who had kidnapped her so they wouldn't do it again," Xena suggested. "Sherlock must not have found that out, so that's why it was a cold case."

"Let's see what Sherlock has to say about it." Xander pulled the large book onto his lap and turned quickly to the right page.

They studied the page, which, as always, was a jumble of drawings, seemingly random words, and what looked like doodles, including some swirly circles. The words "Norwood" and "rattle" appeared above and below the swirls. "Somerset House" appeared under a sketch of a three-story mansion, with "Aha!" next to it. They read "Telegraph office—address?" and finally, there was a sketch of a large sailing ship with something scribbled on its side.

Xena and Xander were used to cryptic notations in Sherlock's notes, but these were even stranger than usual.

"What are all these marks and circles?" Xena asked. "It looks like he didn't have much to write, so he doodled. I don't know, Xander—it's all very confusing." She was usually more cautious than her brother about taking on new cases, but this time even Xander was hesitant.

"There's not a whole lot to go on," he agreed. Then he turned over some pages in the casebook and saw once more the notes their great-great-great-grandfather had made about the missing portrait by the painter Nigel Batheson, the terrifying Beast of Blackslope, and the mysterious Egyptian amulet—all of them cases that Sherlock had had to abandon, and that he and Xena had solved.

"There's something familiar about that

Norwood
rattle
Telegraph office–address?
Somerset House
Aha!

name." He closed his eyes and muttered "Norwood, Norwood" to himself a few times, and then shook his head. "Must be the name of someone at school or a street name or something. Anyway, we can't give up before we even start! We don't even know what the case is yet. Let's see what Alice has to say tomorrow, and then we can decide."

CHAPTER FOUR

Are you sure this is the right place?" Xander stared at the gate. It was made of wrought iron, and the shiny black metal rods twisted into curlicues and rosettes were obviously not just for beauty. They were arranged in such a way that nobody could slide through them, even someone short for his age (as Xander was) and thin (as they both were). Xena and Xander had come up a drive from the street, and after two turns, the gate in the high stone wall and the house behind it had become visible.

If the gate and wall were impressive, the enormous house behind them was mind-boggling. It was painted white and had pale brown shutters at all the windows. Eight columns were lined up on the porch that must lead to the front door. The curving drive opened out in a wide sweep in front of the mansion. Xander imagined cantering up on a noble steed and leaping down onto the gravel, with bowing servants coming out to take his horse and to lead him inside to a grand room where he would be served lemonade and muffins.

"I didn't know there was anything like this in the city," Xena said in a hushed tone. "You could walk right past it and not know it was behind the wall."

They jumped as a man's voice said, apparently right in their ears, "Who is calling?" They looked around, and Xander pointed to a speaker mounted above a camera that appeared to be staring at them with its one black eye.

"Xena and Xander Holmes," Xena said as soon as she recovered.

A pause. "Please face the camera and state your full names."

"Xena Irene Holmes."

"Alexander Mycroft Holmes."

A whirr, and the gate clicked. Xander pushed it open. They had taken only a few steps when someone came hurrying out onto the porch. It was a friendly-looking woman wearing jeans and a sweatshirt, her dark hair piled on top of her head. "Come on in!" she called. "Sorry you had to go through that interrogation." She rolled her eyes and grimaced back at the house as though to tell them she thought it was silly.

"I'm Alice's nanny," she said. "Or I was her nanny when she was a baby, and now I more or less see to her clothes and her schooling and things like that. You can call me Miss Jenny." She held open the big wooden door, and they stepped inside.

"Wow!" Xander said.

"I know," Miss Jenny said. "It's quite grand, isn't it? Not at all homey, I'm afraid. But Alice's family and mine have lived here off and on for generations, when we're not in Borogovia, so we're used to it." She walked them through the cavernous entry room and opened a door that led down a corridor.

"I can't imagine getting used to *this*!" Xena exclaimed, stopping to admire a woven tapestry hanging on the wall. It showed a young man on horseback chasing after a white deer into a forest filled with brilliantly colored birds, foxes, and rabbits.

Xander gaped at an ornate suit of armor. He

tapped on its chest and looked embarrassed at how loud it rang.

Miss Jenny laughed. "I see what you mean, but I hardly notice these things anymore. I grew up here and in Borogovia, like my mother before me and her mother, all the way back to my great-great-aunt, Eugenia Mimsy."

Xander nudged Xena, but she didn't need a reminder that the nanny hired to take care of Princess Stella, the baby who had been kidnapped, had been named Miss Mimsy.

Miss Jenny talked about the house as they continued down the corridor and into a room with a huge fireplace, big chairs covered in red velvet, heavy dark curtains, and an Oriental rug.

"This is the sitting room, built in 1870. It's part of an addition, one of many. The center of the house is among the oldest buildings in London. It survived the Great Fire—you've heard of it?"

"It was in 1666," Xander said promptly. "Most of the city was destroyed."

"Very good!" said Miss Jenny, and she laughed again. She seemed like a cheery person. "Well, the old part is where I live with my husband—he's the family's driver—and our daughter,

Gemma, who's just about your age, I think, Xena. She and Alice have been best friends ever since they were babies."

Miss Jenny opened another door and said, "Hang on, we're almost there!" As he went through, Xander glanced to his right and did a double take at the sight of an open door leading to a park with a fountain and tall, leafy trees. But it was still too early in spring for leaves. What was going on?

"That's one of our famous paintings," Miss Jenny said at his look of amazement. "Go ahead, touch it!" Xander put out a tentative finger, as did Xena, and sure enough, it was a flat wall. "We passed another one earlier. Did you see the marble columns that separated the south drawing room from a library where a dog was sleeping on a cushion?"

"I don't know which was the south drawing room," Xena confessed, "but I did see the dog!"

"What you saw was actually a clever painting of a dog. These paintings are called *trompe l'œil*"—Miss Jenny pronounced it "trump loy"— "which means 'fool the eye' in French. They were very popular in the seventeenth and eighteenth centuries. And here's Alice's study."

Miss Jenny opened yet one more door, and finally, there was Alice. She was sitting at a large desk made of dark wood, with a computer so sleek that Xena longed to get her hands on it. A piano stood near the window, and the shelves were full of books. The far end of the room was set up like a movie theater, with comfortable-looking reclining seats, a screen, and what appeared to be a powerful sound system.

It was hard to imagine anyone who lived here, with this room all for her own, being anything but wildly happy. But the rims of Alice's eyes, when she raised them from the book open in front of her, were red, as was the tip of her nose.

"Thank you, Miss Jenny," she said.

Miss Jenny laid her hand on Alice's forehead. "Still no fever. Are you sure you feel well?"

"I'm fine." Alice made an obvious effort to smile.

Miss Jenny didn't seem convinced, but she said, "I'll leave you to it, then. Give me a ring if you want anything."

"I will." Alice watched as the door closed.

Xena and Xander didn't know Alice well enough to ask what the matter was, but on the other hand, she had asked for their help, so they stood awkwardly in the middle of the room.

They didn't have to wait long. "Something bad has happened," Alice said as soon as Miss Jenny's footsteps had faded into the distance. "Those letters—the ones I told you about—they're gone!"

"*Gone?*" Xena couldn't hide her shock. "You mean like disappeared?"

Alice nodded and blew her nose on a large, lacy handkerchief. "It's more complicated than that. This morning at breakfast, I showed them to my aunt and asked her about them."

"Wait a second," Xena said, and she pulled a small spiral-bound notebook and a pencil out of her schoolbag. "Who else was there?"

"Miss Jenny and Gemma. My bodyguard, Jasper, and the cook and Frieda—she's a new maid and is still in training, so for now she only serves at breakfast until she knows how to do everything right."

"What could be so complicated about serving food?" Xander wondered aloud as Xena scribbled, *Miss Jenny, Gemma, Jasper, cook, maid (Frieda).*

Alice smiled for the first time since they had

come in. "You don't know Borogovia! Everything is bound by customs. It's pretty complicated— you have to eat your salad with a certain fork, and there are some dishes and glasses that only I can use. That kind of thing. That's why I prefer to eat in here with Gemma. But Aunt Penelope makes me have dinner with her and sometimes other meals too, so I'll know how to behave when I go back to Borogovia."

Xena and Xander noticed that she didn't say "when I become queen." It must be strange to think about ruling a country at the age of thirteen, much less talk about it with people she hardly knew, Xena thought.

"So what did your aunt say?" Xena asked, her pencil poised over the paper.

"She read all the letters," Alice said. "It took a while and it was kind of awkward, since no one can get up from the table until she does, and Gemma had to go to rugby practice. When Aunt Penelope finished them, she folded them up and put them in her pocket. I noticed that her cheeks were red and her hands were trembling. She said the letters were nonsense and that I had to stop talking about them. Then I . . ." She swallowed hard.

"Yes?" Xena asked. "Then you what?"

"Then I asked her to give them back to me." Alice seemed shocked at her own daring. "I said that they were written by my great-great-great-grandmother and I wanted them."

"What did your aunt do then?" Xander asked.

"She let Gemma leave for practice and then gave me the letters. I could tell that she didn't want to."

"If they were nonsense, like she said, she didn't really have any excuse to keep them," Xena said. "So she had to give them to you, or it would look like she'd been lying about them."

"That's what I thought too," Alice said. "But I still couldn't get up, and Miss Jenny said something about the Rathonian question. I think she was trying to change the subject."

"The Rathonian question?" Xander echoed.

Alice sighed. "It's this whole thing that's going on in Borogovia. The country next door, Rathonia, is a lot bigger, and they're trying to take over Borogovia. They say the two countries used to be one kingdom and should be united again. Lots of Borogovians agree, but other people say that the only reason they used to be one big kingdom is that Rathonia invaded Borogovia way back in the Dark Ages, and that we've been independent now for five hundred years and should stay that way."

Xena prompted Alice again. "What happened next?"

"Nothing. My aunt dismissed me and Miss Jenny, and I came here to do my homework. I left the letters right here, next to my computer, so I could look up some words."

Homework? Xander thought. On the first day of spring break?

"Then Gemma and I went out into the garden, and I helped her with some rugby drills. I came back in after an hour or so and looked for the letters. But they weren't there!" Alice bit her lip for a moment and then went on. "I asked Aunt Penelope, and she said she didn't know anything about them. I looked everywhere. So did Miss Jenny and Gemma, and even Jasper and Frieda. But I can't find them. Aunt Penelope got angry when I asked her again and said that they were distracting me from my studies, so it's just as well that they're lost.

"But they *were* important because my great-great-great-grandmother wrote them. And I wish I still had them," she finished.

"You read Borogovian?" Xander was impressed. French was his hardest subject. He could memorize all the words in the dictionary, but putting them together in the right way seemed impossible.

"I've had a traditional Borogovian education as well as what I have to learn at LMS. Luckily, the science and math are pretty much the same, but there's a lot of old poetry I have to learn, plus Borogovian and Rathonian history."

"Wow, no wonder you start your homework on Saturday morning!" Xena exclaimed, feeling sorry for her. "You must have tons!"

Alice acknowledged this with a roll of her eyes. "Even with all those lessons, I couldn't really read the letters. The Borogovian language has changed some—even the handwriting is different—and I don't know the formal style too well. They've started teaching it to me in preparation for my coronation, but it's hard. All I could tell was that Queen Charlotte was worried about something, something to do with the baby. Sherlock Holmes"—Xena and Xander exchanged glances—"had asked the queen some questions that upset her. But she never did say what they were. And then he looked all over the baby with his magnifying glass."

"That's weird!" Xander said. "What could he see with a magnifying glass?"

"A birthmark?" Xena hazarded.

"But if you needed a magnifying glass to see it, nobody would know she had one, unless someone had already looked at her with one and discovered it before she was kidnapped, which isn't likely," Xander said.

"There's one more thing." Alice's voice pulled them out of their speculations.

"What is it?" Xena asked.

"She—Queen Charlotte—said one more thing that I kind of understood, but I can't figure out what it means. The letter that talks about Mr. Holmes says that right before he left, he said, 'Things are seldom what they seem,' and then he called the nanny, Miss Mimsy, a flower. I didn't recognize the Borogovian name for what kind of flower it was, so I had to look it up. It's a buttercup. Why would he call her a buttercup?"

"Maybe you read it wrong," Xander suggested.

"I could have," Alice agreed. "But the problem is that I don't have the letters anymore, so I can't double-check the word. That's why I need your help. Aunt Penelope acted so strange. She might have taken them, or told someone to take them. Do you think you can help me find them?"

"Miss Alice?" A deep voice made them jump. Jasper, Alice's bodyguard, was standing in the doorway.

CHAPTER FIVE

Xena scanned the bodyguard's face, but even with her talent for reading people's expressions and body language, she couldn't tell if he had overheard them talking about the letters that Queen Charlotte had written. It was really starting to look as though someone had taken them. Jasper had been present when the letters were discussed at breakfast, making him one of the suspects, so it would be awkward if he knew they were investigating.

Jasper didn't seem to notice he had startled them. He said, "Miss Penelope wishes to know if you and your guests would like your tea in here instead of in the dining room. She is occupied with a visitor and says you may be excused from tea with her if you prefer not to wait until she's free."

"Yes, please." Alice was beet red. Her voice

trembled as she asked her guests, "What will you have?"

"What is there?" Xander asked.

"Anything you like," Alice said.

It must be nice being a princess and being able to order whatever you wanted, Xander thought. "Could we have muffins?" he asked, his mouth already watering at the prospect of the soft, slightly sweet pastry slathered with butter.

"Of course. Xena?"

"Muffins are fine with me."

Alice nodded at Jasper, who gave a slight bow and left.

"How come we didn't hear him?" Xena asked. Her hearing was unusually acute, and normally she would have known when someone was approaching.

"He wears soft-soled shoes," Alice explained. "And he's well trained in being quiet. He might have to sneak up on someone who's planning to hurt me."

"Do you think he heard anything?" Xander asked.

"I hope not," Alice said. "We didn't really say anything, though, did we? I just told you what I read. If someone who can read old Borogovian took the letters, they'd know everything I said anyway, wouldn't they?"

She looked so anxious that Xena hastened to reassure her. But Xena couldn't help worrying that now the bodyguard knew that she and Xander were not there only to record Alice's audition, but also to talk with her about the mysterious letters.

"Who else in the house understands that old kind of Borogovian?" Xander asked.

"I'm not sure," Alice said. "Miss Jenny must. Anyone who knows the modern language and has a dictionary could figure it out if they had enough time. That would mean just about every-body in the house!"

"Including Jasper?" Xena asked.

Alice nodded. "And if he thought there was something worth telling my aunt, he'd do it. He does *everything* she says and doesn't even ask why. He even says he's in favor of Rathonia taking over Borogovia just because she is."

"Why does your aunt want Rathonia to take over?" Xander asked.

"She feels Rathonia will bring prosperity to Borogovia and the royal family, which means her and me. But Gemma told me that she and her mom think we should stay independent. Borogovia fought really hard to separate from Rathonia back in the sixteenth century, and Gemma says that it would be like betraying all those patriotic soldiers who died for independence if we let the takeover happen."

"That's brave of Miss Jenny," Xena said. "Isn't she afraid your aunt will fire her for disagreeing with her like that?"

"Oh, Aunt Penelope could never do that!" Alice sounded shocked. "Women in Miss Jenny's family have been nannies for the Borogovian royal family for more than a hundred years. When Miss Mimsy retired, she brought in her niece from the country to take care of Queen Stella's children and grandchildren. That was Miss Jenny's great-grandmother. Everything in Borogovia is run by tradition. People just wouldn't accept it if my aunt fired Miss Jenny. But my aunt did tell her and Gemma to stop talking to me about the Rathonian question."

"How do *you* feel about it?" Xena asked.

Alice shrugged. "I don't know that much about it. I guess I feel like my aunt does. That's what scares me the most about becoming queen. I'll have to take a stand one way or another when

I make my coronation speech right after the ceremony."

It was hard to imagine Alice making important decisions, but this talk wasn't getting the audition video done. Xena glanced at the clock. "We'd better get started. Your aunt will wonder what we're doing."

Xander had already set up the camera and microphone. "What are you going to sing?"

"I haven't decided," Alice said.

He ran through the titles of some of the songs at the top of the charts, but Alice shook her head again and again. "It's not that I don't like them," she explained. "I just don't know them."

"Well, what music *do* you know?" Xena asked.

"Mostly Borogovian folk songs." Xena and Xander exchanged glances. They didn't remember any contestant singing folk songs, especially in a foreign language. Alice would have better luck with a pop song.

"And some show tunes," Alice added.

"Well, let's try one of those," Xander said.

Alice came around from behind the table. They had never seen her out of her school uniform, and were surprised that on a Saturday, while she was doing homework, she wore an expensive-looking dress, shiny shoes, and a pretty necklace. She put one hand on the piano, and as she prepared to sing, once again the change in her was dramatic. She threw her shoulders back, and she almost seemed taller. Her face shone, and her lips parted in a confident smile.

Alice launched into a song that sounded vaguely familiar to Xena and Xander. She came to the end, and it was hard for Xena not to burst into applause until Xander had turned off the recorder.

"That was *great!*" Xena said.

Alice turned pink again, this time from pleasure, and flopped into one of the poufy chairs. "Do you think so? It's from one of my favorite musicals, *Annie Get Your Gun*."

The door opened again, but instead of Jasper, a tall woman came in. She would have been pretty if it weren't for the scowl that had worn lines around her mouth and eyes. She wore a long dress and high heels, and her hair and nails gleamed. Xena suddenly felt sloppy in her comfortable weekend clothes.

Alice jumped up and smoothed her dress. All

the confidence she had shown a few minutes ago disappeared as she stood uncertainly. "Aunt Penelope," she said, "I'd like you to meet my friends, Xena and Xander Holmes."

"Xander? What kind of name is that?"

"It's short for Alexander," he said.

Alice's aunt either didn't hear him or didn't care what he said. She turned to Xena and asked, "You're the children who are related to that detective?" She said "that detective" the way someone else would say "that burglar" or "that swindler," and both Xena and Xander became indignant. Xena, standing behind Xander, touched him lightly on the shoulder to remind him to keep his temper, then said, "Yes, ma'am. Sherlock Holmes was our great-great-great-grandfather."

"Ha!" Aunt Penelope said. "Not so great as all that!"

"No, that's how many greats," Xander said. "He was our father's father's—"

"What I mean," the woman said, as though addressing someone who wasn't very intelligent, "is that he wasn't as great a detective as everyone thought he was. As some people still think he was."

"He was too!" This time it was Xena who needed restraining. "Just because he couldn't solve—" She stopped short before she blurted out *because he couldn't solve Princess Stella's kidnapping,* and instead finished lamely, "He couldn't solve all his cases because sometimes he was called away on something more important by the queen or the prime minister. *They* trusted him."

"He was a very odd man," Alice's aunt went on, as though she hadn't heard Xena. "Most foreigners are. Borogovian ways are very ancient and traditional. Foreigners will never learn them, and will never be able to understand why it's important for us to ally with our neighbor Rathonia. And now it is time for you children to go. Her Highness has a great deal to do."

Xander turned his back on her and packed up the recorder. Xena saw that he was about to explode, so to cover, she thanked Alice for her hospitality. Alice stammered something about how they were welcome anytime, and then Jasper came in to lead them out. Xena stuffed her notebook back into her schoolbag and followed him.

They didn't notice the amazing paintings or

the beautiful rooms this time. Jasper hurried them through the corridors and the chambers, and almost before they knew it, they were standing outside the gate, which clanged shut behind them.

"Well! Can you believe *that*?" Xena was shaking with anger.

Xander said, "And to top it all off, we didn't even get any muffins!"

CHAPTER SIX

Xena and Xander rode the Tube home from Alice's house in silence, still fuming. Xander was too full of angry energy to sit. He stood the whole way, holding on to a strap and imagining cutting remarks he could have made to Alice's aunt to make her stop insulting Sherlock Holmes, yet which wouldn't be so disrespectful that he'd get in trouble. Xena kept remembering how miserable Alice had looked. She didn't think that Alice's aunt hit her; surely the nasty woman wouldn't dare touch someone who would someday be her queen. But the royal house, beautiful and full of marvels as it was, seemed cold and hard. And as they rode the clacking train and then went into their small but warm and cozy apartment, cluttered with furniture that was showing wear after their months in London, she felt sorry for Alice.

Xander commandeered the computer and downloaded Alice's audition. She had barely stayed within the thirty-second limit dictated by the rules of *Talented Brits*, so he trimmed the opening and closing. Xander manipulated the recording to make it look like he had zoomed in on her face a few times when she was looking especially expressive, and then pulled back to show her whole body swaying to the music.

"Xena!" he called. "Come look at this!"

He heard her exclaim "Darn!" from her bedroom. She came out holding a schoolbag. "Look what I did! I was in such a hurry to get out of there before I yelled at that awful woman that I grabbed the wrong schoolbag. Now I have Alice's and she must have mine."

"You'll have to go back there tomorrow and swap them. That new phone Mom is testing is in there, isn't it?"

"*Double* darn!" Xena had forgotten about the phone.

"And you know what just occurred to me? Why did Alice's aunt mention Sherlock to us, and the whole thing with Rathonia? It had nothing to do with what she was talking about. Do you think she was spying on us and heard us talking with Alice about Rathonia and the kidnapped baby? Or maybe that Jasper guy was eavesdropping and told her. It's weird that she'd bring it up out of the blue."

Xena considered this. "Maybe. I hope he doesn't tell Alice's aunt that Alice thinks she might have taken the letters." She hated when people eavesdropped on her.

"I'm going to call my cell and see if Alice answers, so we can get the right schoolbags," she said. "Can I use your phone?"

Xena's phone rang until she was sure that the voice mail was about to pick up, but finally Alice answered.

"Hello, Xander?" Her voice was tentative.

"It's Xena. I'm calling from my brother's phone. I think I got your schoolbag by mistake."

She heard papers rustling, and then Alice said, "Yup, this one isn't mine. Mr. Frank—he's Miss Jenny's husband—is busy getting ready to go out of town until Monday, but he can drive it over to you then. Would that work?"

"It would for my homework, but the phone is something my mom is testing. It's an experimental one, and the company she works for is really paranoid that someone will get their hands on their new stuff and copy it. Can I come tomorrow and get it?"

"Oh, yes!" Alice sounded so happy about another visit that Xena felt guilty for not picking up on how lonely she was and offering to come over without the excuse of the phone. "And Xena . . ." Alice hesitated, then continued, "Would it be okay if I used your phone for a little while?"

"Sure, it has unlimited texts on it, so go ahead. When should I come over tomorrow?"

"Whenever you like." She lowered her voice. "I wanted to tell you something anyway, and I didn't want to have to wait until school was back in session."

"Can you tell me now?"

Xander looked up, alerted by something in his sister's voice.

Alice hesitated again, and then said, "Okay. My aunt asked what you were doing here and I told her about the audition video, and she got *really* mad. She said that I had gone behind her back and someone in my position can't go onstage in front of a lot of people and make a spectacle of herself." Xena heard that Alice was holding back tears. "She said that even if the judges of

Talented Brits call me in for a live audition, she won't let me go."

"Oh, wow, Alice." Xena was at a loss for what to say. "I'm really, really sorry we got you in trouble."

"It wasn't your fault. You and Xander were so nice to help." Alice took a ragged breath. "Later, I went to look for her. Sometimes she changes her mind, although she always says I misunderstood her the first time. She would never admit to being wrong. She was in the parlor—you know, that room with the blue wallpaper?"

Xena had seen so many rooms that she didn't remember which one was which, but she said yes to encourage Alice to go on.

"She was talking to someone. I was just about to knock when I heard her say something about Princess Stella."

Xena froze. Princess Stella? The baby who had been kidnapped? "What did she say?"

"I didn't hear that part. But then she said, 'If people knew the truth, things would be quite different. We must make sure that no one ever finds out.'"

Xander went around the table. He gestured to Xena to hold the phone away from her ear so that he could hear, but it was already too late. Alice's voice dropped to a whisper as she said, "Someone's coming!" Suddenly there was no one on the other end.

Xena closed the phone slowly and handed it to Xander. "What was that all about?" he asked, and she explained.

"I want to go with you tomorrow," he said. "Something's going on that we need to check into." She nodded, too worried to answer.

They were quiet at dinner, and when their parents suggested watching an old movie together on TV, they said "Sure" without enthusiasm. Their dad popped popcorn, and they all piled onto the couch. The movie turned out to be funnier than they had expected, and for a while they forgot about Princess Stella, Borogovia, and Alice's unpleasant aunt.

When the movie ended, their dad reached for the remote, but their mother said, "Let's just watch the beginning of the news. The kids don't have to go to bed right now—they have the week off."

"Some people have all the luck," their father pretended to grumble.

The announcer came on and said the transit

strike had started that afternoon, just after Xena and Xander had gotten home from Alice's.

"Phew!" Xena said. "What if we had been stuck out there? But how can we get back to the mansion tomorrow?"

"I can take you in the afternoon," their father offered. "I want to get some work done in the morning while I'm fresh."

Xena didn't see how they could stand to wait until the afternoon. She couldn't help feeling worried about Alice.

"Mom?" Xander turned his big blue eyes on their mother. Even she was known to cave sometimes when he turned on the charm.

"Sorry," she said. "I have a brunch appointment with friends on the other side of town. I won't be back until mid-afternoon. Looks like your dad is a better bet."

The next morning, they were up early, even though they had both been woken up more than once by thunder that sounded as though it was crashing right down on their apartment building. It was still pouring when their dad came into the kitchen to refresh his coffee. Xander asked, "Is this a good time for you to take a break?"

He switched on the radio and shook his head. "Sorry, son. I'm just hitting my stride."

Xander was about to beg when Xena said sharply, "Hush!" Xander was going to tell her that she couldn't boss him around when he realized what the announcer on the radio was saying. "Princess Alice of Borogovia has vanished from her London mansion. Preliminary reports indicate that she has run away, perhaps overwhelmed by the pressure of her upcoming coronation. Police are at the mansion, investigating the disappearance.

"Tomorrow's weather—" But they weren't listening. They turned to each other and stared wordlessly.

Xander finally broke the silence. "Alice? *Disappeared?*"

CHAPTER SEVEN

As soon as their father heard that Xena had Alice's schoolbag, he said, "I'll finish my work later. We have to take it to the mansion so the police can see if they can find anything helpful in it." In the car, he turned on the radio and tuned it to a news station. He had to raise the volume above the *swish-swish* of the windshield wipers when the rain started again.

Xena hadn't noticed anything unusual when she had rummaged through Alice's bag, but then, she hadn't been looking for clues. On the way to the mansion, she and Xander, seated together in the back, pulled out the textbooks, notebooks, pens, and other ordinary things that everybody carried to school. They leafed through the pages of the books, but nothing fell out.

"What's this?" Xander pulled out a small bound book. Xena tried to grab it but he held it out of her reach. "Nuh-uh! I was the one who found it."

"What is it?"

"A calendar." He turned over the pages.

"That's kind of personal," she said. "Maybe you shouldn't read it."

"The police are going to look at it," Xander said reasonably, "and they don't even *know* Alice."

"Well, hurry up then. We're almost there."

Xander flipped to the week before. On Friday was the notation "Audition after school" in Alice's neat handwriting, then some school assignments. On Wednesday was written "G's birthday!!!" The notation "my birthday" on the following Saturday was written in much smaller letters, and with no exclamation points.

"Who's G?" he asked.

"Must be Gemma, Miss Jenny's daughter," Xena said. "They're really good friends, don't you remember?"

"Here we are," their father said from the front. "Would you look at that!"

They looked up from shoveling Alice's things back into her schoolbag. "Wow!" Xander said.

The sidewalk in front of the mansion's drive was packed with reporters and photographers, and uniformed police holding them back. There wasn't an inch of space on the curb. "I don't suppose either of you brought an umbrella?" their father asked. Xena and Xander shook their heads and he sighed. "Get out here and tell the officer what you have. I'll find a place to park and be right back."

Somehow, Xena managed to squirm through the crowd. She popped out from between two closely packed bodies and nearly fell at the feet of a police officer.

The officer grabbed Xena's elbow. "Careful!" she warned, and added, "You shouldn't be here. There's nothing to see, and you'll just get in the way."

"But I have evidence!" Xena held the school-bag up. "This belongs to Alice!"

"How long are they going to make us sit here?" Xander asked. He and Xena were waiting in a small room—if any room in that mansion could be called small; this one was almost as big as their whole apartment—while their father talked with the police. "And why are they asking Dad about the schoolbag? He doesn't know anything. They should be asking us!"

Xena sighed. "That's how grown-ups are. They think that kids don't know anything."

They looked up as the door opened, but it wasn't the police or even their father. It was a girl about Xena's age. She had dark wavy hair, a snub nose, and freckles. She looked from one of them to the other. "Are you Xena and Xander Holmes?" They nodded. "I'm Gemma. You met my mom yesterday—Miss Jenny. She sent me in here to keep you company."

"Do you know what happened to Alice?" Xena asked.

Gemma's light brown eyes clouded over. "Nobody does. She just—just disappeared."

"When did someone notice she was gone?" Xena wished she had brought her notebook with her. Xander's memory wasn't any better than anyone else's unless he read something, and they might be getting some good clues.

"About eleven o'clock last night. Did you hear that thunderstorm?" Xena and Xander nodded. "Alice is afraid of thunder. That's how my mom found out she was missing—at the first thunder-clap she went into Alice's room to see if she was frightened. When she didn't find Alice in her bed, she thought maybe she'd gone into my room, but she hadn't. So my mom alerted the security team and woke up Miss Banders, Alice's aunt."

"What makes them think Alice ran away?" Xena asked.

"Miss Banders found a note."

"What did it say?" Xander asked.

"I don't know. They won't let me see it. My mom said the police took it."

As though they had heard themselves being mentioned, two police officers came into the room, accompanied by Mr. Holmes. "Xena and Xander Holmes?" one of the officers asked, glancing at his clipboard.

Xena and Xander stood up. "Yes, sir," they chorused.

"What do you know about the young lady's disappearance?"

"Nothing," Xena said. "We were going to come here today to trade her schoolbag for mine. I picked up hers by mistake when we were here yesterday."

The police asked them a few more questions and seemed disappointed when Xena and Xander couldn't supply them with any more information.

"Can I have my schoolbag?" Xena asked after the police told them they were free to go.

One of the officers nodded. "I think I saw it in her bedroom. I can have someone fetch it for you."

"Please, let me get it myself," Xena said. "I think Alice took some things out of it, and I need to make sure I have all my schoolbooks so I can do my homework over break." This wasn't strictly true. Alice hadn't said anything about taking books out, but on the other hand, she was so conscientious about her homework that she might have used one or two of Xena's until she had her own back.

The officer said, "Well . . ." and appeared to be thinking about it.

Xander looked up at him with his most appealing smile. *"Please?"*

The officer smiled back and said, "All right, then. I'll accompany you." Xena wondered what would happen when Xander grew up a little— would he still be so cute that adults couldn't refuse him anything?

"I'll go with you," Gemma volunteered. "I know where Alice puts her things."

"I'll get the car and meet you at the gate," their father said. "That way only one of us will get wet."

Alice's bedroom was huge, as they had imagined, and very grand. Still, there were little homey touches about it that kept it from being formal and cold. A framed photograph of a laughing woman holding a baby sat on the dresser. "That's Alice's mother, Queen Juliette," Gemma said when she saw Xena looking at it. "She and the king were killed in a plane crash when Alice was just two." Some ragged stuffed animals were on top of the bookcase, which was filled to overflowing with books. All expensive hardcovers, Xander noticed.

"Is this yours?" One of the policemen held up a navy schoolbag decorated with a crest showing the head of a giraffe, their school's emblem.

Xena looked inside the bag. She saw the science lab notebook with her name on it and a few other things. "My math book is missing, and a book I was supposed to read for literature class." She looked around. "There's the math book." She pointed at the desk. "Can I get it?"

The policeman nodded. "Just don't disturb any of the powder." Xena and Xander didn't have to ask about the powder that lay in a white mist over all the hard surfaces. They knew that it was for finding fingerprints. Xena picked up the math book carefully, and saw the novel she was supposed to read, so she took that too. A glass jar on the desk caught her eye. It had several banknotes in it—seventy pounds or so, she guessed, about a hundred dollars. Odd that Alice would leave that behind if she was running away. Wouldn't she need money? But then, a princess probably got a huge allowance, and seventy pounds wouldn't mean much to her.

"Is that all?" the officer asked.

"I think so—" she started, but Xander interrupted her.

"What about your cell phone?"

"Oh, right!" She'd forgotten all about it. She looked inquiringly at the policeman.

"We didn't find one."

"Are you sure?" He shook his head, and Xena's heart sank. She would get in a lot of trouble if her mother found out she didn't have that phone.

On the stairs, Xena asked Gemma if Alice had a lot of pocket money. "Hardly any," Gemma told her. "Her aunt says it isn't good for her to have more money than other people, but she gets even less than I do." Xena opened her mouth to ask about the jar on the desk, but changed her mind.

Their father wasn't back yet, and Alice's aunt was talking with some police officers. "Can you hear what they're saying?" Xander whispered to Xena, who shook her head.

"I'll try to find out." Xena was an athlete and took her studies of martial arts very seriously. She had the ability to move smoothly and silently, and she often managed to get close to people without being seen. Her mother called it "Xena's cloak of invisibility," and it had helped her in past investigations. Xena crept as close as she dared, keeping her eyes down—she had learned long ago that a direct gaze attracts attention—until she was standing next to a table polished to such a deep sheen that it cast back her ghostly reflection. She paused.

"I understand you have quite a complicated security system here," one of the officers was saying. "I saw your camera outside. Have you reviewed the recording from last night?"

"The system was knocked out by a lightning strike," Alice's aunt said. "We didn't discover this until long after my niece had disappeared."

"Who was in the house, ma'am?"

Xena crept a bit closer.

"Mrs. Giles—Princess Alice's nanny—and her daughter, Gemma, and the princess's bodyguard."

The policeman looked up. "No other servants?"

Xena leaned over the table.

"No. The servants had all been given the night off."

Xena let her eyes stray over the papers on the table. They mostly looked like official forms, but then her eye was caught by a piece of the familiar three-hole paper with faint blue lines that everyone used for schoolwork. Part of it was covered by another paper, but the first words let her know what it was.

Dearest Aunt Penelope,
Don't bother looking for me because I
don't want to come back.

It was the note that Alice had left. For a moment Xena thought of picking it up, but that would have meant circling around the table and getting closer to the police and Alice's aunt, and she wasn't confident of remaining unseen. She was pretty sure that neither the police nor Aunt Penelope would be willing to let her read the note, but the more she thought about it, the more curious she became. So as carefully as she could, she glided back to where Xander and Gemma stood watching her.

"Give me your phone!" she said to her brother. Normally he would object to her bossing him, but he could tell from her urgency that this was not the time to protest. He handed it to her, and she moved slowly back to the table.

Xander watched as she reached across the table and slid a piece of paper off another one. He held his breath, hoping that none of the adults would notice his sister. He didn't know what she wanted with his phone until he saw the flash of the camera. It must have caught the eye of Alice's aunt, too, because she turned and snapped at Xena, "What are you doing? Are you in the pay of those dreadful newspapers?"

"No, ma'am, I—"

"Give me that camera!"

"But I—"

This time Xena was interrupted not by Alice's aunt, but by a commotion at the door as a short man in a black suit burst into the room. She retreated to stand next to Xander and Gemma and handed the phone back to her brother, hoping Miss Banders would forget about it.

"Who's that guy?" Xander asked Gemma.

"He's the Borogovian prime minister," Gemma answered. "He arrived in London last night to help Alice rehearse for the coronation. He brought Alice's crown and other things that she'll need."

"Any news?" the man asked.

"Nothing, sir," one of the officers said. The man collapsed in a chair and buried his face in his hands. "Don't worry, sir," the policeman said. "We'll find her."

The prime minister lifted his head. Dark circles were under his eyes, and his hair stuck out as though he hadn't combed it that morning. "Thank you. I'll do whatever I can to help. Why do you people allow transit strikes? Even the— what do you call that tunnel between England and France? Oh yes, the Chunnel—even the Chunnel was closed. I had to hire a private boat to bring me over from the Continent, and we just barely made it into the port before that storm closed down the shipping for small boats. There was construction work outside my hotel last night, so I hardly slept, and then it was almost impossible to find my way here."

"Calm yourself," Alice's aunt said.

He turned to her as though seeing her for the first time. "And then someone tried to break into my hotel room last night!"

"What?" The policeman pulled out his notebook again. "What happened?"

"I told hotel security that someone was on my balcony," he said. "They sent up a man to check. He said nobody was there, but I distinctly heard someone. I must have scared him off."

Xander couldn't restrain a little snort of laughter at the thought of a burglar being scared by this small, round-eyed man in his pajamas.

As the prime minister went on and on, complaining about the thunderstorm, the traffic-clogged roads, his concern over Alice's disappearance, Xena observed him carefully. Was he as worried as he appeared, or was it an act? She had a feeling that he was hiding something. She focused on what he was saying. Maybe he would give it away, whatever it was.

"What time did you arrive in London?" the police officer asked the prime minister, interrupting his flow of words.

"Late last night." He waved a hand dismissively, as though details were beneath him. "I don't know exactly at what time. What a dreadful situation! What will I tell my people?"

"Xena!" She turned around. Her father was standing in the doorway, dripping all over the beautiful rug.

"Are you still here?" Aunt Penelope turned on her and then glared at Xander. "Out! Now!" she spat, and they scurried out the door.

It was raining even harder now, and their father was soaking wet. He turned up the heat in the car, muttering under his breath as he pulled away from the curb.

Xena explained to Xander why she had needed his phone. "There's something strange about Alice's note, but I don't know what it is. Let me see your phone again." The image was too small to see clearly, and she handed it back to him.

"There was something else strange," Xander said. "If you were going to run away from home, what would you take with you?"

"Money," Xena said. "I noticed that too. If Gemma's right, Alice didn't have much, so she would have taken everything out of that jar on her desk."

"Right. And wouldn't she take that picture of her with her mom?"

"Obviously that picture was important to her," Xena said. "It was right up there on her desk where she could see it every day. Plus, my cell phone was gone."

"Wouldn't she take it if she ran away? She doesn't have a phone, remember?"

Xena shook her head no. "I don't know Alice very well, but I bet she would never steal anything, even if she needed it badly. Someone else must have my phone. And I don't think she ran away. Where would she go? She doesn't have any other relatives, right? I don't think she's friends with anyone at school who would hide her. She's close to Miss Jenny and Gemma—would she leave them without a word, especially right before Gemma's birthday and the glee club performance? And what about *Talented Brits*?"

"Okay, okay!" Xander held up his hand. "So if Alice didn't run away, what do you think happened to her?"

"There's only one other possibility."

"You mean . . ."

Xena nodded. "I think Alice was kidnapped!"

CHAPTER EIGHT

They got home before lunch. Normally, during vacation, they would just be getting up at this hour, but they were so worried about Alice that they were eager to tackle the problem of her disappearance first thing.

As soon as they were inside, their father said, "I'm going to change into some dry clothes and then go to the university. I might be able to get some work done there. You two okay on your own until your mom gets back?"

They assured him that they were.

"So why did you want to take a picture of that paper?" Xander asked as Xena downloaded the photo to the family computer and then enlarged it.

She shook her head in frustration. "I'm not sure. There's something about it that looks—I don't know, wrong."

Together, they read the note.

Dearest Aunt Penelope,
Don't bother looking for me because I
don't want to come back. I'm very sorry
to hurt your feelings by leaving, but I
have to do it. I don't want to return to
Borogovia, and I don't know how else to
stay here.

Love,
Your niece, Alice

"It's short and kind of formal," Xander said, "but I don't think writing notes like that is something you practice for, is it?"

"Aha!" Xena said. She jumped up and ran into her room, and then came back with some pages stapled together. "This is the science project that Alice and I worked on together last term. Does the handwriting look the same to you?"

Xander looked from the school paper to the note. He hesitated. "I don't know," he finally admitted. "It kind of looks the same, but some things about it are different. Do you think Alice didn't really write that note?"

Xena was already dialing the phone on the

desk. "Dad? I think something funny is going on at Alice's house." She explained, then waited. "Okay. Where is it?" She hung up and turned to Xander. "Dad says it's probably nothing, but we should show the picture and the project to the police. He told me where the police station was." She pressed PRINT and waited while the cell phone picture printed out, and then made a copy of a page of the project. "You know what it means if Alice didn't really write the note, don't you?"

Xander swallowed. "It means you were right. She was kidnapped."

"So what makes you kiddies think that two different people wrote these?" The policeman at the desk tapped the printout of the photograph.

"Look at the way she crossed the *T* on her homework and the way it's crossed on the note. They're different. Plus, the capital *A* is different, and—" Xander looked up at a snort from the policeman.

The man was trying not to smile, without much success. "A couple of amateur sleuths, are you? Good for you! Maybe when you grow up you can join the force and be real detectives." He gathered up the papers and said, "I'll see that these go to the . . . er . . . to the proper channels."

There didn't seem to be anything else to say, so they thanked him and left, ducking under awnings to keep out of the pouring rain. The wind made their umbrellas almost useless.

"I bet I know what he means by 'the proper channels.'" Xena was bitter. "I bet he'll throw them right in the trash. Good thing we didn't give him the original of the class project."

"He's just like Inspector Lestrade," said Xander.

"Who?"

"A policeman who never believed Sherlock, no matter how many times he was wrong and Sherlock was right."

Back home, they read the note again. "I just don't believe it," Xena said. "Even if Alice didn't want to leave London, she seemed pretty convinced that she had to become the queen."

"Maybe whoever wrote it couldn't think of any good reason for her to run away and this was the best they could come up with," Xander said. "Hey—why don't we send this and a picture of the homework project to Andrew? The SPFD is sure to know someone who can analyze handwriting."

Xena faxed them to Andrew with a note explaining what was going on. It felt good to be actually doing something. Xena and Xander hadn't known for very long that Sherlock Holmes was their great-great-great-grandfather, but once the SPFD had given them his cold-case notebook and they started detecting, they realized that they had been born for this.

"Okay," Xena said. "Time to try to figure out who—who took her." She didn't even want to use the word "kidnapped." It was too scary.

"If that was the only note they found"—Xander indicated the bogus message—"that means there wasn't a ransom note. Right?"

"Right. So the motive can't be money. Do you think it's just a coincidence that she disappeared so soon after she found the letters? Could the letters have something to do with why she's gone?"

Xander considered this for a moment. "Maybe," he finally conceded. "But what? Do you remember what Alice said about them?"

Xena thought back. "Not much. There was something that worried her, she said, about when they talked about the baby. And Sherlock was mentioned. Not much more than that."

"Maybe it has nothing to do with the baby. Maybe there's something else in the letters that would make a difference in her coronation—like they changed the age someone had to be when they were crowned or something. The one thing we know for sure is that someone took them. The letters wouldn't have just disappeared in the short time she was doing those rugby drills. So let's work on them. Who knew that Alice found them?"

Xena read from her spiral notebook, "Aunt Penelope, Miss Jenny, Gemma, Jasper, the cook, and a maid named Frieda."

Xander chewed his lip. "That's a lot. Alice said they could all probably read the letters. And any of them might have talked. The servants might have friends in town, or relatives, or any of them could have told the postman, who could have told someone else on his route."

"No way," Xena said. "The kidnapper had to be someone who was known and trusted, or they couldn't have gotten into the mansion. There's that bodyguard and the security system. Remember the camera at the gate? If that Jasper guy isn't involved, he wouldn't let the mailman or anyone else in. It has to be one of the people on our list."

Xander wasn't so sure. He thought that orderly Xena sometimes relied too much on lists. But all he said was, "Let's find out more about Borogovia, especially about the kings and queens. You can check online, and I'll look in the history books in the study."

"What are we looking for?" Xena asked.

"Anything unusual. Not all that stuff about how many square miles it is and the annual average rainfall."

After an hour, they assembled their findings. Xena read the list she had made in her notebook. "One: In the seventeenth century, Borogovia was really torn up by wars of succession, between different people claiming they should be the next king. The wars were so bad that when they were finally settled, the Borogovians wrote a new constitution that said that whoever is crowned king or queen is the legitimate ruler, even if later on they figure out that actually someone else should have been crowned. No do-overs." She looked over the top of the notebook at her brother. "Did you read about those wars in one of the books?"

He nodded. "This king—his name was Carl—died in 1632. He didn't have any kids, so normally his younger brother would be the one to take over. But his brother had died before him, so the brother's son said *he* was king. The problem was that Carl also had a sister, and she said that *she* was queen. There was no law against a woman taking over, but it had never happened before, and a lot of people said that it should be Carl's nephew instead."

"So what happened?"

"There were two different wars and a lot of people died in them, including Carl's nephew, so Carl's sister became queen. Then someone found some old legal document that said women couldn't rule, so there was *another* war to try to get rid of her and have a male ruler. The queen's side won, and they were the ones who made the constitution that said once someone was crowned, that was it."

"Got it," Xena said. "Two: Just barely more than half the Borogovians want to stay independent from Rathonia. There was a poll a few months ago, and it was fifty-one percent to forty-nine."

"Hmm. So if a new queen said one way or the other about it, probably at least a few people would change their minds."

"Right. And it wouldn't take more than a few people to make a difference when it's that close. Three: Lots of Borogovian rulers have married English people. Alice's mom was English, and so was Princess Stella's. They built the mansion right after the wars of succession, and it's been enlarged lots of times. The most recent time was when Queen Charlotte—she was Stella's mother, remember?—was homesick, and she added a whole story so her family could visit. Some famous architect made it. A newspaper article from the time said, 'It is a marvel of both engineering and architecture.' "

"What does that mean?" Xander asked.

"Engineering means how it was made, like how strong it was, and architecture means how it looked. So I guess that means it was well built and beautiful."

Xander sighed. "I didn't find anything more than that. All this is interesting, but I can't see how it helps us find Alice. Let's take a look at the casebook. Oh, and I thought of something—you know those glass cases in the lobby of the SPFD where they display clues that Sherlock used?" Xena nodded. "Well, one of them holds things that are all about the kidnapping of Princess Stella."

"Do you remember what they were?"

He squinted. "Um, a picture—like a family photo. I guess that was the princess. And a kind of pin—it was a black flower behind glass, like a tiny picture. I didn't look too closely. We'll have to go back so I can—"

His phone rang. "Hi, Andrew. You already heard back?" He said to Xena, "Andrew has the results of the handwriting analysis." He spoke into the phone again. "Wait, let me put you on speaker so I don't have to tell Xena everything you say."

"—can't be sure without seeing the originals," said Andrew's voice, "but he would be really surprised if the two samples were written by the same person. I'm faxing you the report."

Xena stood by the fax machine. When the report came through, she scanned it quickly and handed it to her brother. He read aloud, " 'Less than a five percent chance that the two samples were written by the same hand,' " and then a lot about capital letters, slant, and other details. "So whoever wrote the note *wasn't* Alice!" He gave the page back to Xena, who tucked it into her schoolbag. "Do you think the police suspect the same thing we do?"

"There was nothing about it on the news sites I checked while you were reading those encyclopedias," Xena said. "So either the police didn't look at the evidence we brought them, or they're keeping quiet about it. Sometimes they do that with important investigations, don't they? I mean, not give out all the details, so they can catch the bad guy when he knows things that only the guilty person would know?"

"I guess so." Xander didn't voice what he was thinking, and he knew that Xena was thinking the same thing.

If the police weren't going to do anything with this important evidence, it was up to them to find their friend.

CHAPTER NINE

Thank goodness for spring break!" Xander said on Monday morning as he and Xena walked to the back of the Dancing Men, a pub near the hotel where they had stayed when they first moved to London. As they had discovered months ago, the long corridor behind the pub's dining room led to a concealed entrance to the headquarters of the SPFD.

"I know," Xena said as she opened a dark brown door, revealing a dusty room filled with empty cardboard boxes that were scattered and stacked in a way to make any visitor think this was a regular storage room. "This case is really complicated. We'd never have time to investigate it if we were in school today."

Xander ducked down and crawled through the false cardboard box that was against a wall. There was a door hidden in the back of this "box," and he quickly spun the dials of the lock to the right combination to let them in.

Xena wasn't crazy about tight spaces, but each time she went through the box and out the door, it was a bit easier. Still, she was always relieved when she climbed out the other side and into SPFD headquarters.

Mr. Brown, a longtime member of the SPFD, looked up from his desk. "There you are! I was wondering how you two were going to get here. It took me almost an hour on my bicycle instead of ten minutes on the Tube."

"Our dad dropped us off on his way to work," Xander said. "His spring break isn't until next week."

"Andrew is fetching the papers about the Borogovian case from the archives." Mr. Brown stood up and pulled a large key ring from his pocket. "And in the meantime, let's take a look at the artifacts that your illustrious ancestor collected."

Xena and Xander glanced into the display cases that lined the wall in the corridor between the lobby and the offices and labs of the SPFD. In one, an ostrich-feather fan with what looked like a bullet hole through its handle drooped over two silk gloves, one of which had six fingers. Another case held a stuffed rodent the size of a cat with a neatly hand-lettered label saying "SUNDAMYS INFRALUTEUS." Its bared teeth were long and yellow, and Xander shuddered and swerved a bit to avoid walking right next to it. He knew the creature wasn't alive, but he still hadn't completely conquered his phobia of wild animals.

Mr. Brown worked a slender key in the opening of the third case. The glass door swung open.

"This is the picture I was talking about," Xander said, pointing at a black-and-white photograph of a sleeping infant. "And there's that flower thing." He reached in and picked it up carefully.

"What is it?" Xena asked. What looked like a tiny oval picture frame of gold held a strange rose, shiny and completely black, even the stem and leaves.

"That's a mourning pin." Mr. Brown beckoned to Xena to look at it more closely. "They were popular a hundred years ago and more. They're made from the hair of someone who died, and were worn in memory of the dead person."

"Yuck." Xena wrinkled her nose.

"I know, it seems odd now," Mr. Brown said, "but people from different times show their grief in different ways. This one was made from the hair of Queen Charlotte's mother, Princess Stella's grandmother."

"She was Alice's great-great-great-great-grandmother," Xander said.

"Right. See, there's a note that came with it."

The spidery handwriting was difficult to read, but Xena managed to decipher: "For Mr. Sherlock Holmes from HRH Queen Charlotte of Borogovia, in gratitude for his efforts on behalf of my late mother's only grandchild."

"It's strange," Xander said.

"To make a dead person's hair into a flower and then wear it, you mean?" asked Xena.

"No, I mean it's really strange that there would be two kidnappings in the same family a hundred years apart. Royal families have bodyguards, servants, lots of people around them. Wouldn't they be the *last* people to be kidnapped?"

"You'd think so," Mr. Brown said, "but actually, royal families are threatened with kidnapping a lot. That's why they have so many bodyguards."

"Everybody around Alice knew about the kidnapping of Princess Stella," Xander suggested, "so maybe when they had to get rid of Alice for some reason, kidnapping occurred to them. Plus, just after Alice showed her aunt and the others at the breakfast table the letters that mentioned the kidnapping, the letters disappeared—and then that same night, she did too. We're trying to find a connection."

"I'll leave that up to you," Mr. Brown said. "I'll see what's keeping Andrew and send him here." He went back to his office.

"So what do you think, Xena?" Xander asked. "What do we do now?"

Xena considered. "I don't know. We can't investigate Alice's disappearance without cooperation from the police, and obviously we're not going to get that. If we solve Sherlock's case, maybe we can figure out what upset Alice's aunt so much when Alice asked her about the letters. That could help us find Alice."

"I don't know," Xander objected. "It's a long shot, and Sherlock's notes are even harder to understand than usual. I mean, what does a ship have to do with anything?"

"The ship that the king and queen were on

when the baby was kidnapped?" Xena guessed, but she knew this was weak.

Xander shook his head. "I don't know how that would help, unless Sherlock thought the king and queen were involved somehow. That doesn't really seem likely. But let's work on it a little. So far we've only looked at that brooch. What else did Sherlock save from the investigation? Anything that could help? We don't have much to go on. There are lots of clues, but none of them seem related to each other."

They examined the other objects in the case. There were some small photographs, chosen for display to visitors of the SPFD to show the most important people involved with the kidnapping. There was one of an uncomfortable-looking Sherlock with the queen, and a few of the princess growing up.

"The little girl looks a lot like Alice," Xena said, and Xander agreed. "Look," she went on, "here's one that says it was taken right after Princess Stella was born. See, the label says, 'Her Royal Highness Princess Stella, held by Miss Mimsy, with her parents seated together in front of them.' " The nurse, her light hair pulled back into a severe bun, stood behind the queen, who looked pale and weak, even in the old-fashioned photograph that didn't exactly bring out the best in anyone. Both women wore dresses with wide, puffy skirts. The king, dressed in a dark suit, held his wife's hand and stared at her instead of looking at the camera, concern evident on his face.

"Why would you call someone who looks like that a buttercup?" Xander wondered aloud, remembering what Alice had read in the letter from Queen Charlotte to her friend. Miss Mimsy was a dumpy little woman, not at all flowerlike.

Andrew finally appeared with a cardboard box full of loose papers. "I don't think you'll find anything here," he said. "They were all catalogued a long time ago, and if anything useful had been mentioned, somebody would have noticed it." By now, Xena and Xander knew that Andrew could be grumpy and discouraging, so they didn't remind him that sometimes they could see a clue that other people missed. Besides, if Sherlock hadn't thought these papers were important, he wouldn't have saved them.

Xander's phone rang. "It's Mom," he reported to Xena. "She's through with her errands and is waiting outside to take us home."

Xander held the door open for Xena as she carried the box past Mr. Brown's office, calling out, "Thanks! Bye!" as he waved at them. They pushed it through the false box in the back of the pub, and then Xander carried it down the corridor and past the curious gazes of people having lunch, and ran with it through the drizzle to the car.

As soon as they were back in their apartment, their mother shut herself in her office to write up some reports and to inspect the gadgets that had just arrived. Xena dumped the contents of the box onto the dining room table. "You start going through the papers," she told Xander, counting on her brother's speed-reading ability to sort through the documents and identify which ones could be helpful. "I'll try again to figure out what some of the notes in the casebook mean."

She left the old notebook open next to her while she booted up. Once online, she checked "Somerset House." The name had seemed familiar when she read it in the casebook, but she couldn't place it. She found it easily on the Internet. It turned out to be one the few museums in London that their mother hadn't taken them to. Xena clicked on "About Us" on the museum's Web site. The original palace had been built in the seventeenth century, just like the Borogovian mansion. Could there be some connection there? She didn't see how. The museum used to be a duke's private palace. It had been rebuilt in the eighteenth century and now had art galleries, music programs, and films, and in winter there was a great-looking skating rink. It must be an interesting place, Xena thought, but what does any of this have to do with Sherlock Holmes or a missing princess? She decided to leave it for the moment and see if any of the other clues were more helpful.

The next thing to figure out was that drawing of the ship in the casebook. Xena wasn't too familiar with boats, but even to her, this one looked old-fashioned. Didn't they have steamships by the late nineteenth century? This one, the one Sherlock had sketched, had lots of sails. Did Sherlock suspect that someone had taken the princess away on a ship? Why would they do that, and then come right back and return her?

Xena leaned in closer and realized that what was written on the ship must be its name.

She got Xander's magnifying glass and read *H*, then *M*, then *S*, then a long word. What was it? She squinted. Why did Sherlock have to write so small? Aha! It said "H.M.S. *Pinafore*." She wasn't sure what a pinafore was—an article of clothing, she thought. She looked it up in an online dictionary. It was something like an apron, and girls used to wear them to keep their clothes clean. The dictionary showed a picture from *Alice's Adventures in Wonderland* to illustrate it.

But the princess who had been kidnapped was much too young to wear something like that, and there were no other little girls in the household, as far as she knew. Maybe Xander had turned up something in the papers—perhaps there was a niece visiting, or a young servant. Just as Xena thought of Xander, he sneezed.

"More musty old papers," he said. "I wish I wasn't allergic to them." He carefully picked up a yellowed sheet, examined it, and added it to a stack. "There's nothing useful here. It's just a bunch of notes, like bills, and contracts with servants and security guards and that kind of thing. Nothing important."

"There must be some reason why Sherlock

saved them," Xena reminded him. "Let's go through them once more."

Xena began to look through the yellowed papers. She felt a moment of hope when she found a copy of a birth certificate for the baby, but it didn't say more than the fact that it was a girl named Stella, and they already knew that. There were bills from the workmen who had refurbished the palace, as well as blueprints for the addition built by King Boris and Queen Charlotte. The maze of white lines and arrows and notations on the architectural drawings meant nothing to Xena. "This isn't getting us anywhere." She was exasperated. "What's that?" She pointed to another paper, which Xander had set aside. He leaned over her shoulder and sneezed again, this time almost right in her ear.

"Yuck!" she said. She closed the box of documents so that the musty smell would stay contained, and handed him a tissue.

"This one's kind of interesting," Xander said. "It's a contract between Queen Charlotte and the nanny, Miss Mimsy. It must have been a pretty bad job. The nanny couldn't do *anything* but take care of the princess. She had a half day off once a week, but the rest of the time, she had to be with the baby, night and day. She wasn't allowed to get married and couldn't even have a boyfriend. Here, this is what it says: 'As is customary, you will not marry while in my employ, as you might be tempted to allow your duties to your own family to interfere with your duties to mine.' Miss Mimsy didn't have her own room but shared it with the princess. She couldn't even make friends with the other servants."

"How long had she been working for the queen when the baby was born?"

Xander examined the paper. "It looks like the queen interviewed Miss Mimsy a few months earlier, when she settled in London to watch over the remodeling of the mansion. Miss Mimsy started work the day after the baby was born."

"What else did you find out?" Xena asked.

"There are some newspapers from when the baby was kidnapped. This article is about when the king and queen got home and found that the princess was back. It says, 'Nobody had seen her being returned, but in their joy, the means of her abduction and her return did not seem important. A few days later, though, the king decided that the fiend who had taken his only child might attempt to do so again, for who knew what nefarious purpose, and so they employed the famous detective Mr. Sherlock Holmes to try to discover the perpetrator.' "

The thought of the terror that the king and queen must have felt, and their confidence in Sherlock, made Xena and Xander more determined than ever to solve their case. But could they succeed at this when the police didn't seem able to do anything? If Xena and Xander had failed in one of their earlier cases, it would have been disappointing, but at least nobody would have been really harmed. It was one thing to find a missing painting or an ancient amulet, or to track down a beast in the English countryside—all things they'd done in the past. But it was quite another thing to look for a missing friend who seemed to have been kidnapped.

"Lunch!" their mother called from the kitchen.

"Did you see anything else in those papers?" Xena asked her brother as they sat down to chicken soup.

"There were some other contracts. The Borogovian king and queen had a *lot* of people working for them! There was a first upstairs parlor maid and a second upstairs parlor maid, and a butler, and a whole crew of gardeners and cooks and security guards."

"Anything more about the baby, I mean."

"There was something about Miss Mimsy. She said she really loved the baby and was terrified when she was kidnapped."

"I bet she was!" Xena said. "If she hadn't been sleeping so heavily, whoever took Stella wouldn't have been able to get away with it."

"Something I don't get, though," Xander said. "If Miss Mimsy was drugged, how could she run to the telegraph office so soon? Wouldn't it have made more sense to send someone else? Maybe she wasn't drugged at all, just pretending! She could have put that opiate thing in her cup herself after she drank most of the cocoa."

"Why would she do that?"

Xander shrugged and blew on his soup.

Their mother joined them. "How's the case coming?"

"Okay, I guess." Xena was not feeling optimistic. "Sherlock's notes are even harder to understand than usual."

"Like what?"

"Like there's a sketch of a ship," Xena said.

"It's one of those ships with lots of sails. The king and queen were on a ship, but what does that have to do with anything? It must be just a doodle. There's a name written on the side of it, but that doesn't make any sense either."

"What's the name?" her mother asked.

"It says 'Pinafore.'"

"Oh, as in Little Buttercup?"

Xander froze with his spoon halfway to his mouth. Sherlock had called Miss Mimsy a buttercup! "What do you mean?" He lowered the spoon carefully back into the bowl.

Their mother launched into song. "I'm called Little Buttercup, dear Little Buttercup, though I could never tell why!"

Xena and Xander's first reaction was relief that none of their friends were there to hear her—aside from it being a strange song, their mother couldn't carry a tune, a fact that their musician father teased her about frequently. Their second was curiosity.

"Who's Little Buttercup?" Xena asked. "And where did that song come from?"

"You mean you've never heard of Gilbert and Sullivan?" They shook their heads, and their mother rolled her eyes. "What *do* they teach kids in schools these days?" She sighed. "W. S. Gilbert and Arthur Sullivan were two men who wrote comic operas in Victorian England. The operas were hugely popular at the end of the nineteenth century, and people still put them on today. Buttercup was a character in their most famous operetta, *H.M.S. Pinafore*. I don't remember much about her except that she sold things to the sailors onboard the *Pinafore*— tobacco, scissors, watches, that kind of thing."

"Wow!" Xena said. "Thanks, Mom!"

"Does that help?"

"I don't see how right now," Xena admitted, "but at least we know what Sherlock was talking about."

"Anything else? I might not have Sherlock's blood in my veins or a photographic memory, but there are some things I've picked up in all my many years!"

"Can't think of anything," Xena said. She and Xander finished their lunch and loaded their bowls and spoons into the dishwasher. Xena wiped down the kitchen table, and by the time she went back into the living room, Xander had already pulled the papers out of the box again and put them next to the open casebook.

"Look at this," he said, handing a yellowing paper to Xena. "It's from a police interview with Miss Mimsy."

Xena quickly scanned the handwritten questions and answers. "Huh!" She put the paper down. "So Miss Mimsy had studied to be an opera singer! I wonder if that has something to do with the drawing of the ship, since it's got the same name as that operetta. What do you think?"

Xander shook his head. "I don't think so. It says that she was in music school, but her family lost all their money in the Panic of 1893, whatever that was, so she had to become a nanny. She worked for some aristocratic families before Queen Charlotte hired her. She had good recommendations from the other people she worked for, including a countess." He rummaged around. "The letters are here someplace."

Before he found what he was looking for, his phone rang. His eyes met Xena's. Could it be Alice?

"Hello?" His face fell, and he looked at Xena and shook his head. She felt her shoulders sag. "Oh, really?" Xander went on. "Okay. No, nobody knows. What day did you say? I'm sure she'll be back by then. Yes, I have your number. I'll tell her to call you as soon as I see her."

He snapped the phone shut. "That was someone from *Talented Brits*. They said that Alice passed the first audition, and they want her to come to the live audition next week."

"Don't they know she disappeared?"

"Duh! It's all over the news!"

"What are you two arguing about?" Their father had come in.

"We're not really arguing," Xena said. "It's just that this case is so frustrating. The clues are so weird! There's something in the casebook about the *H.M.S. Pinafore*, but it doesn't seem to have anything to do with the princess."

"Are you sure?" their father asked. "What have you found out about the operetta?"

"Not much," she admitted.

He disappeared into the study and came out with an encyclopedia of music. "The Net isn't the best place to learn everything, you know." He leafed through the book and began reading them a synopsis of the story. It was hard to follow and kind of unbelievable, and they exchanged glances. Trust their dad to get excited about something so silly!

" 'Little Buttercup and the captain,' " their father read, " 'then sing a duet entitled "Things Are Seldom What They Seem." ' " Xander raised his eyes in a question to Xena, and she nodded vigorously. Those were the exact words that Sherlock had said to Miss Mimsy!

"Sorry, Dad," Xander said. "Could you start over from the beginning?"

"Sure!" He seemed pleased at Xander's interest.

It turned out that the operetta was complicated, with people falling in love with other people who weren't of the right social class for them to marry. Buttercup wasn't a major character at the beginning, but she became important when it turned out that she had been a kind of foster mother to two of the men in the story when they were little boys, and she accidentally switched them, and somehow that led to everybody being able to marry all the right people.

Their father snapped the book shut. "Got what you needed?"

"I don't think so, but thanks anyway."

"And what about the other clues?" Xander asked.

"What other clues?"

"You know, like those circle things in the casebook."

"Those are just doodles," Xena said. "And those other words—'Norwood' and 'rattle'—there isn't enough there for me to investigate online. There must be at least a hundred hits for each of—" She broke off when she realized that Xander wasn't listening. He got to his feet and went to the bookcase, where he pulled a fat volume off the shelf. Xena recognized it as being Dr. Watson's famous accounts of Sherlock's solved cases. Xander turned the pages without hesitating and mutely held the page up where Xena could see it.

" 'The Adventure of the Norwood Builder,' " she read. "So why didn't you remember this before, Mr. Photographic Memory?"

"It's just like you and the computer," he retorted. "Norwood is a pretty common name. I knew I'd seen it before, but I didn't know where, exactly, until it came to me just now."

"What was the case about?"

Xander scanned the pages to remind himself. "I don't think what the case is about is so important," he said. "It's one of the clues in it that Sherlock must have been thinking about."

"*What* clue?" Xena felt like strangling him.

"Fingerprints!"

"So?"

"Look at those swirls again."

Xena examined the casebook page. "You know, they do kind of look like fingerprints!" Xena typed something on the keyboard. "Okay, it says here that in Sherlock's time, the police knew that all people have different fingerprints, but in England they weren't used as evidence in crimes until 1901, when Scotland Yard set up the United Kingdom Fingerprint Bureau. When was the kidnapping again?"

"December 1894."

"So then why would Sherlock be interested in fingerprints?" Xena asked. "They couldn't have records of criminals' fingerprints if the government didn't even start keeping track of them until *after* the princess's kidnapping. They wouldn't have anything to compare with the fingerprints he found."

Before Xander could speculate, his phone beeped. He pulled it out of his pocket and saw that he had a text message. Without much interest, he glanced at it, and then sat up straight. "It's from your phone! It must be Alice!" He opened the message and then wordlessly showed it to Xena: "riting u while noones here took me up 2 the"

Then it stopped, as though the sender had to hastily press SEND before finishing. Xander frantically punched buttons to call her back, but instead of Alice's timid "Hello?" he heard his sister's voice telling him to leave a message. He sent back a text message saying, "where r u?"

"What is it?" Xena asked.

"She must have turned off the phone." Xander was glum.

"Or someone else did."

"That would mean someone caught her at it. Someone who doesn't want anyone to know where she is. Someone—"

"Someone who knows now that we're on the case," Xena finished for him. Neither one spoke what was in their minds. Would the ruthless kidnapper come after them next?

CHAPTER TEN

So you kiddies think the message came from the missing princess?" Two days had passed since they had talked to the police about the handwriting in the note that was supposedly from Alice, but unfortunately, once again the same officer was at the desk. His tone was polite, but Xena detected a smirk in his voice. They explained again, and the officer opened Xander's phone, looked at it in bewilderment, and handed it back to Xander. "Show me what you saw."

Xander found the message and passed the phone back to the man.

"This makes no sense," the officer said, and this time it wasn't a smirk but irritation that both of them heard clearly. "And here, what's this?" His large fingertip covered the screen.

"I can't see where you're pointing." Xander tried to sound polite.

"It looks like the sender was someone named Xena." He looked hard at both of them. "Didn't you say that was your name, young lady?"

"Yes, but—"

"Unusual name, wouldn't you say? Not likely there are two Xenas sending messages to this lad's phone."

"But—"

"And," said the policeman, as though in triumph, "the princess's name is Alice. Not Xena, is it?" He snapped the phone shut and handed it to Xander. "You kids must have something better to do than to play tricks on the police. Did you ever hear of interfering with an investigation?" He held up a finger for silence as Xena was about to say "but" again, and she clamped her lips shut. "It's a serious offense, but I have kids of my own, so I won't report you. Not this time, anyway. However, if you poke your noses into this again . . ." He didn't need to finish the sentence.

"I told you, he's another Lestrade," Xander said glumly as they made their way through the Tuesday-morning crowds. It wasn't full tourist season, but London was never completely free of foreigners who stood hunched over maps as they tried to figure out where they were going. Xena and Xander made their way around two young women and overheard one say to the other, "No, it's here—see? Waterloo Bridge. It's right next to that."

"I don't understand why he won't pay attention to us," Xena said. "It's not like we were making things up. He's just like most grown-ups—he doesn't get texting at all. Just because it was sent from my phone doesn't mean I'm the one who sent it!" She waited for a response from Xander, but there wasn't one. She looked around and saw that he had stopped and was talking to the two women. He was exercising his famous charm, flashing his blue eyes at them, making the most of the dimples that appeared whenever he smiled.

"So it's too far to walk?" one of the women asked.

Xander nodded. "It's a short Tube ride, but there's no Tube today. I can try to get you a cab," he offered.

They both said, "How sweet!" and he went to stand on the curb, where Xena joined him.

"What are you doing?" she asked. "We're in the middle of an investigation!"

Xander looked smug. "They said they were going someplace near Waterloo Bridge."

"So?"

"So that's where Somerset House is! We still haven't figured out what Sherlock meant by writing that in the casebook. Let's go there and see if we can find something out."

Even on a day when people were almost fighting over taxis, Xander managed to snag one. The two women thanked him profusely, and he said, "Mind if we come along? We need to go that way too."

"Of course! Hop right in."

The drive took longer than usual due to the heavy traffic, and Xena and Xander made polite small talk with the two women. They were from Australia and were eager to see everything. When they got out of the taxi, the two women went to a nearby shop while Xena and Xander stopped to gawk at the huge palace that was Somerset House.

"What amazing fountains!" Xander said. They paused in the courtyard to watch as the brilliant jets of water shot up in the air and danced in intricate patterns. Xena wandered over to look at some signs standing against the elegant, immense building.

"Wow, I'd love to come back sometime and see this!" She pointed at a notice about an exhibit of works by William Shakespeare.

Xander shrugged. He wasn't as interested in old things as his sister was, and besides, there wasn't time. He approached the information counter.

"Six pounds each, please," said the man seated there.

Xena and Xander looked at each other. Neither had that much money on them. Most museums in London didn't charge admission, and it didn't occur to them that they might need to pay an entrance fee. "We don't need to see the exhibits," Xena explained. "We were just interested in the history of the building."

The man directed them to a room off the courtyard that was devoted to the history of the palace. Xander immersed himself in old engravings showing the palace when it was a private home.

"Check this out," Xena said from across the room. Xander tore himself away from a scene of elegant ladies with parasols walking small dogs on leashes across a bright green lawn. Xena was looking at a long text detailing what had happened to Somerset House once it had become a public building.

"This has got to be why Sherlock was interested," she said. "See, it says that this is where they used to store all the birth certificates and marriage licenses and things like that for the whole country."

Xander rapidly read the rest of the information. "It says that during Sherlock's time, anybody who wanted information about British subjects could go to Somerset House to find whatever it was they were interested in. This could be why Sherlock mentioned it in the casebook! He might have wanted to know something."

"But what?"

Xander was reading again and didn't answer. "Darn it," he muttered.

"What?" He didn't answer, so she read it for herself. "Oh."

The records—all 300,000 of them—had been moved to the National Archives when Somerset House became a museum.

"So where are these National Archives now?" Xena asked.

"A long way away." Xander had memorized the map of London. "This says they're all the way in Kew." Xena didn't know where Kew was, but from Xander's tone, it wasn't anyplace they could walk to, and the chances of lucking on someone going that way in a taxi again were slim. What tourist would be interested in birth certificates and marriage licenses?

"Time to call the SPFD." Xander pulled his phone from his pocket.

Mr. Brown pulled up to where they were waiting on the curb. They settled themselves into his comfortable car and he drove to Kew, in the southwestern part of London. Mr. Brown kept them enthralled with his tales of the work he had done as a young man with the CID, the detective branch of Britain's police force.

"Did you ever work on a kidnapping?" Xena asked.

"One or two, but they were much different from this. I can't go into detail, you understand." Mr. Brown dropped them off, saying he was picking up Andrew from a friend's house and he'd be back for them in an hour.

The huge glass-and-cement complex of the National Archives could hardly be more different from the graceful stone Somerset House. The buildings were kind of intimidating, but Xena and Xander found some comfort in the way they looked. They clearly meant business.

Once again, there were posters advertising exhibits of old manuscripts, letters to and from famous people, and other records of all kinds. Xena promised herself she'd come back as soon as she could. She tore herself away and followed Xander, who was striding toward the information booth.

She caught up with him just as the man at the desk was saying eagerly, "Oh, so you're the kids who are descended from Sherlock Holmes! I've always loved his cases, and I followed the ones you were involved in with interest. What are you working on now?"

"We can't talk about it," Xander said.

"Oho, state secret! Well, fill out this form, and I'll help you locate what you need."

Xena filled in the blanks, requesting any papers in the five years leading up to the kidnapping of Princess Stella bearing the names of Queen Charlotte, King Boris, Princess Stella, or Miss Mimsy. She pushed it over the counter to the man, whose eyes widened.

"This will take a while." He handed the form

to a clerk. "You can look around, if you like. I'll call your name when we have something."

They were too nervous to do anything but pace up and down the corridor, looking at the large pool outside and glancing up at the high ceilings. It was a quiet place, like a library, except when someone came in and exclaimed over the building and the exhibits.

It seemed like forever before the man's voice said, "Holmes?" They hurried back to the desk. "I've put the documents you requested in a private reading room. Here, put these on before you handle them." He handed each of them a pair of white cotton gloves. "Oils from your hands can damage the pages. You can have room three-twelve."

The room was almost bare, with a table and two chairs, and a glass door in sight of the main desk. Xena was dying to get her hands on the papers, but she knew Xander could speed-read them so fast that there was hardly any point in her helping. So she sat on the hard wooden chair in the small, windowless room, chewing the inside of her cheek nervously.

"Aha!" Xander held up a yellowing sheet of paper. "Got it!"

"What is it?" Xena tried to snatch the paper out of Xander's hand, but he said, "Nuh-uh! You might rip it."

He spread the paper out on the table. At the top, it said in flowery writing, "Certificate of Marriage." It was dated June 1892 and the groom was Jonathan Blunt, which meant nothing to Xena, but the bride's name was familiar: Eugenia Mimsy.

"Miss Mimsy got *married*?" Xena could hardly believe it. "But the contract said she wasn't supposed to!"

"She was married before she became a nanny, and I guess she didn't want to tell the queen. And look at this!" Xander pointed to the words "birth certificate" scrawled in the margin, in the by-now familiar handwriting of their ancestor Sherlock Holmes.

"So Miss Mimsy had a secret marriage a year and a half before she went to work for the queen." Xena copied the names and dates into her notebook. "Good for her. I know it wasn't honest, but it's not fair that she couldn't have her own family when she was taking care of someone else's. And we know that Sherlock found this same paper. I wonder what he meant by 'birth certificate.' This is a marriage license."

"I don't see where this takes us," Xander said. "Lots of people must have had secret weddings in those days, if nannies couldn't get married. And look at this." He showed her another paper, a death certificate for Jonathan Blunt, dated only a few months before his wife was hired by the queen.

"That must be why Miss Mimsy—or Mrs. Blunt—needed the job so badly that she'd lie," Xena said. "Hmm . . . I wonder."

"You wonder what?"

Xena shook her head. "Never mind. It's crazy. Unless . . . wait a second. Don't leave this stuff. I don't want someone to think we've left and clean it up." Xena ran out. Through the glass door, Xander saw her conferring with the clerk, who nodded and disappeared into the back. What was she doing?

In a few minutes, the clerk came back and handed her another piece of paper. Xena scanned it, raised her head, and asked the clerk a question. He went back into the archives. This time he stayed away for so long that Xander was about to get up and see what was going on, when the man reappeared, empty-handed this time, and shook his head. He and Xena spoke together a little longer, and then she came back.

"What's that?" Xander tried to snatch the paper from his sister's hand.

Xena couldn't hold back a triumphant smile. "A birth certificate for the nanny's baby."

"What?" This time he managed to grab it. Sure enough, it said that in November 1894, a baby girl named Josephine was born to Eugenia Mimsy Blunt, widow of Jonathan Blunt.

"Think about it, Xander. The queen interviewed Miss Mimsy—or Mrs. Blunt—months before Princess Stella and Josephine were born. If the nanny didn't tell the queen that she was married, maybe there was something else she wasn't telling her. Like, that she was going to have a baby."

"What made you think that?"

"Remember what Sherlock called Miss Mimsy?" Xena asked.

"You mean 'Buttercup'?"

Xena nodded. "And remember what we found out about Buttercup in the opera?"

Xander sighed in exasperation. Usually he was the one who tantalized Xena with hints, and he wasn't used to having to guess. "She sold things to sailors, and she used to be a nanny, and she took care of two babies who—" He broke off as understanding dawned on him.

Xena nodded. "Exactly."

CHAPTER ELEVEN

Buttercup used to be a nursemaid," Xander said, "who took care of two babies. One of them became the captain of the *Pinafore*, and the other became a sailor."

"Right." Xena opened the glass door of the reading room. It was getting stuffy in there, with no window and the two of them breathing the same air. "But earlier, Buttercup had mixed the babies up and for some reason never told anyone."

"Maybe that's what Sherlock was getting at when he called Miss Mimsy 'Buttercup,'" Xander said. "Do you think the princess who was returned wasn't the same baby as the one who disappeared? You think someone switched them, the way you and Alice switched schoolbags?"

"I don't know—but I'm beginning to think

that Sherlock thought so. And it also looks like he had a suspect: the nanny. That would explain why Sherlock said 'Things are seldom what they seem,' " Xena said. "Everyone just assumed that the baby who was returned was the same one who had disappeared. But she wasn't."

"So that's why the nanny pretended to be drugged, and she didn't really send a telegram," Xander said. "The longer nobody saw the baby, the better."

"Right! Remember how Aunt Lou said she wouldn't have recognized you, when she saw those photos Mom sent her from the park? And it had only been a few months since the last time she saw us. When the baby came back after a month, people might have thought she looked different, but they'd think it was just because babies change a lot, even more than people our age."

"So that's why Sherlock was interested in fingerprints," Xander said. "He wasn't trying to find the *criminal* with fingerprints—he was trying to see if this baby was the same one who had been kidnapped!"

"What?"

"Think about it, Xena. Why else would he be interested in the *baby's* fingerprints? Remember the word 'rattle' surrounded by the drawings of fingerprints? He must have found a toy rattle that Princess Stella had used before the kidnapping, and was trying to figure out if the baby that was returned had the same fingerprints. That could be why he examined her with a magnifying glass!"

"It makes sense," Xena agreed.

"I wonder how Miss Mimsy snuck the baby out," Xander said. "Remember, I saw contracts with security guards."

"You could easily hide a little baby under one of those huge skirts they wore. She must have been really afraid the baby would cry."

"Why did you ask the guy at the desk to go back into the archives after he found the birth certificate?" Xander asked.

"I wanted to see if there were any more records about Josephine Blunt."

"And there weren't?"

"Nope." Xena shook her head. "But he also said that a lot of records were lost during World War Two, when buildings were bombed. If Josephine lived out in the country, any record of her marriage or death could have been destroyed. So we don't know for sure what happened to her."

"Anyway, if Miss Mimsy did switch them," Xander said, "she certainly didn't want anyone to know that she had her own baby—she'd be sure not to leave a paper trail. She must have been relieved when the queen had a girl too. If it had been a boy, she wouldn't have been able to make the switch."

"Do you remember when Princess Stella was born?" Xena asked.

Xander closed his eyes and called up the birth certificate in his memory. "November 1894."

"Just the same age as Josephine," Xena said. "It must have been really hard for Miss Mimsy to leave her newborn baby with someone else. Maybe she came up with this switch as a way to keep the baby near her."

"What do you think Miss Mimsy did with the real princess?"

Xena thought a moment. "Remember that when she retired she brought her niece in from the country to be the next nanny?"

"You think that was the princess, and not

really the nanny's niece at all?" Xander asked eagerly.

"I bet she was! That would mean that the baby who got 'returned,' the one they all thought was the princess who had been kidnapped, was really Josephine Blunt, not the princess at all!"

Xander's eyes sparkled. "And Miss Mimsy's great-great-granddaughter, Miss Jenny, is the real heir to the throne."

"Which means that Miss Mimsy's descendant is Alice! Remember, one of the newspaper articles said that the nanny wanted to be a singer!" Xander exclaimed. "Maybe that's where Alice's musical talent comes from, the way we inherited detecting skills from Sherlock."

"And the blond streak in our hair from Mom."

"Right!" Xander was excited. "If Miss Jenny is the real heir to the throne, then Aunt Penelope won't be a relative of the queen. You can tell she wouldn't like that. She likes being the boss of everybody. I bet the letters say something about the babies being switched, or at least the queen's suspicions that something like that happened, and Alice's aunt took the letters from Alice to destroy them. She must know about the switch, and she's trying to prevent the truth from coming out."

"Maybe," Xena agreed. "But Sherlock would never jump to conclusions like that. We still don't have any proof that it was Aunt Penelope who took the letters—or Alice. What if the prime minister knew about the switch too, and he's holding Alice for the same reason? Or what if Miss Jenny is holding Alice until she can proclaim herself queen? Maybe she's showing the letters to the prime minister. He could *also* be the kidnapper. Or Jasper, or even the cook or the maid!"

Just then, a loud *bang* came from outside. "What was *that*?" Xander asked as they ran into the corridor. They joined the crowd that was gathering at a window.

Security guards ran outside and poked around the courtyard. One of them held something up. "Kids!" said the archivist who had helped them. "Just a firecracker."

There was nothing more to see, so Xena and Xander returned to their study room. Xena picked up some loose papers and looked under them, and then crawled under the table.

"What are you doing?" Xander asked. "We don't have much time. Mr. Brown will be back any minute."

"The birth certificate!" Xena sounded desperate. "Josephine Blunt's—it's gone!"

CHAPTER TWELVE

Xena and Xander were waiting anxiously, fingers crossed that there was another copy of Josephine Blunt's birth certificate. "Sorry," the man at the desk said when he returned from his search in the archives. "It's expensive converting all those documents to electronic files. I'm afraid that the documents you were interested in just weren't important enough."

"Thanks for looking," Xena said, and Xander added, "Yeah, thanks." He sounded so disappointed that Xena didn't have the heart to nudge him to remind him to be more polite.

"Will you let us know if it turns up?" she asked.

The man nodded. "I have your names and phone numbers here." He tapped the form they had filled out to get the documents.

Xander glanced at his phone to check the

time. "Mr. Brown is probably waiting for us outside," he said. "Thanks again."

Outside the archives building, Andrew waved to them from the window of Mr. Brown's car. Xena and Xander filled him in on the case, and then told both Andrew and Mr. Brown what they had found out and about the disappearance of Josephine Blunt's birth certificate.

"If we don't have it, then nobody will ever believe us about the baby," Xena concluded.

"Someone must have thrown that firecracker as a diversion and then taken the document." Mr. Brown's voice was grim. "I want you kids to be more careful. It looks like someone knew you were there. I think you're being followed."

Xena swallowed around a sudden hard lump in her throat. "Okay, we will." She was struck by the chilling thought of the danger they might be in. If they interfered with the kidnapper's plans—whatever they might be— Alice's kidnapper might get angry and come after them. Xena tried to put it out of her mind, but she resolved to keep a close eye on her brother, who tended to dash into risks without thinking.

She forced herself to speak lightly. "Do you

remember what the birth certificate said, Xander?"

"Yes, I do—names and dates and everything. Good thing the person who took the birth certificate doesn't know about my photographic memory! Still, it's all just a theory. We can't prove anything now."

"What can't you prove? That Alice isn't really the princess?" Andrew snorted from the front seat. "That's easy."

"Easy? How would *you* do it?" Xander asked. Andrew always rubbed it in when he knew something they didn't, but this time Xander didn't care if Andrew acted all superior, just as long as he could help them prove their theory.

"Didn't you ever hear of DNA analysis?"

"Yes," Xena said cautiously. "I've heard of it, but I'm not sure what it means."

"It means that if you have a part of somebody's body, like hair or a fingernail or even some spit or something, a scientist can compare it to a part of somebody else's body and tell if they're related."

"But we don't have a part of Princess Stella's body," Xander objected, "or any part of Alice's body."

"We have that pin!" Xena exclaimed. "The mourning pin with Stella's grandmother's hair! Could we use that, Andrew?"

"I think so. I'll call the expert and see." He pulled out his phone. "Hello, Aunt Mary?" Mary Watson was another member of the SPFD. "Can you connect me with Dr. Crichton?" After a few minutes, he was explaining the situation. "Okay. Right, got it. How long? Any way to speed that up? All right, I'll tell them. Cheerio." He turned to Xena and Xander. "Dr. Crichton says that she can use a small piece of the hair in the pin and compare it with something of Alice's."

"I hope they can do it pretty quickly." Xander was anxious. "Alice's birthday is in four days."

"I can ask them to put a rush on it," Andrew said, "but I don't know if they can hurry it along at all."

"How can we get something of Alice's?" Xena asked. "I suppose her hairbrush and things are in the house, but how can we get them?"

"Gemma would give them to us," Xander said. "But the phones there are bugged, remember? If we tell her what we're doing, then Alice's aunt and her bodyguard and who knows who else will hear about it."

"Who's Gemma?" Mr. Brown asked. They explained. "Leave it to me. I'm sure I can get in touch with her mother through the embassy."

He pulled over to make a phone call, but before he could take the phone out of his pocket, Xena said, "Wait!" Mr. Brown paused. "How do we know Gemma's mother isn't involved?"

"Miss Jenny?" Xander was surprised. "It couldn't be her! Remember how nice she was?"

"We've seen nice people do bad things on our other cases," Xena reminded him. "If we're right about the baby switch, then she's the one who would be the queen of Borogovia. That's a really powerful motive. She could say she won't do it for some reason, or she could give us some-one else's hair or baby tooth or whatever."

"What do you want me to do?" Mr. Brown asked.

"Let me think." Xander buried his face in his hands. After a moment he looked up again. "Okay. How about this—ask her for a few things of Alice's, like a shirt she's worn and a hairbrush. We can tell Gemma that we're getting a dog to track down Alice."

"That would never work," Xena broke in. "We can't just turn a dog loose in the middle of

London and tell it to find Alice! If we knew she was someplace specific, we could go there and use one of those dogs, but it would be hopeless without that information."

"Exactly! Miss Jenny has got to know that too. If she has nothing to do with the kidnapping, she'll give us the things even if she doesn't think they would help. But if she *is* the kidnapper, she'll be glad to give them to us and let us waste our time instead of doing anything really useful."

"Okay, Xena?" Mr. Brown asked.

"You could try," Xena said. They waited.

Mr. Brown got on his phone. "Get me the Borogovian embassy, please, Mary." A pause. Then Mr. Brown explained that he urgently needed to speak with someone named Jenny in the Borogovian mansion. Another pause, and then he passed the phone to Xena. "It's your friend's mother on her cell."

By the time they had reached central London, Miss Jenny had agreed to send Gemma to the SPFD with some of Alice's things. "My husband can drive her there. Anything to help get Alice back."

• • •

Gemma was waiting for them outside the pub that concealed the entrance to the SPFD. She was thrilled at the secret door that let them in. "That was the most fun way to get into a building I ever saw!" she said. "I wish there were a secret entry to the mansion! I hate knowing that I'm being watched on those silly cameras every time I go in or out."

She handed Andrew a plastic bag with a school uniform and a hairbrush in it. Xena and Xander saw with satisfaction that some long blond hairs were embedded in the bristles.

"My mom doesn't think this will work," Gemma said. "She's really upset. I found her looking at an old video of me and Alice when we were little, and she was crying. She said she'll never forgive herself, and that she should have been keeping a closer watch on her. I tried to tell my mom that she couldn't sleep in the same room with Alice, but I don't think that made her feel any better."

"We'll keep working on it," Xander promised. "We already have some clues. Has there been anything else at the house—a ransom note or a threatening phone call or something?"

Gemma shook her head. "Nothing. I'll call

you if anything happens." She got up to leave.

"Wait a second," Xena said. "There's a bug in your hair."

"Ew!" Gemma reached up a hand but Xena grabbed her wrist.

"Let me get it." She pulled at something on Gemma's scalp and the girl jumped. "Sorry! I didn't mean to pull out that hair too."

"It's okay," Gemma said, rubbing her head. "Just as long as you got that bug! Give us a ring if you find out anything, will you?"

"Of course." Xena felt guilty about tricking Gemma, but she had no choice. "And there was something I wanted to ask you. I heard Alice's aunt say that the servants had been given the night off, the night of the kidnapping?"

Gemma looked surprised. "They usually get Friday evenings, but Miss Banders had them switch to Saturday. I don't think she said why." Xena and Xander exchanged glances. It sounded like Alice's aunt had wanted as few witnesses as possible to what she was going to do that night.

Gemma's phone chirped, and she glanced at it. "My dad's outside," she said. "Please call me right away if you find something out, okay?"

"We will," Xander promised.

"Thanks for your help!" Xena called after her as Mr. Brown walked Gemma out to the sidewalk.

"What was that all about, with the bug in her hair?" Xander asked his sister when Gemma was out of earshot. "I didn't see any bug!"

Xena handed Andrew the hair she had pulled from Gemma's head. "I think we need to get Gemma tested too." Andrew left to pack it separately from Alice's blond ones and get them delivered to the DNA lab. "It just seemed awfully convenient that all the servants were out that night," she said. "We can always confirm with the security tape that they actually did go out, if we need to, but it looks like they were sent away on purpose." She took a deep breath. "Let's try to narrow down the suspects. First, if the cook and Frieda really were out, and Gemma's dad was out of town, who else can we eliminate?"

"Let's look at motive," Xander suggested.

"I keep coming back to the letters," Xena said. "Alice found them, she talked about them in front of all the people who are now suspects, and then *poof*! The letters are gone. And then that night, *she's* gone."

"Let's assume that something in them triggered Alice's kidnapping," Xander said. "But what?"

"The only thing we know about them is that they're about Princess Stella's disappearance and Sherlock's investigation," Xena said.

Xander drummed his fingers on the table. "Could the timing of the kidnapping have something to do with the fact that she's going to be crowned soon?"

"I'm not sure." Xena, as always, was a little more cautious than Xander at drawing conclusions. "Anybody who cares about Borogovia knew that Alice's birthday was coming up, and she'd be the queen right after that. They could have taken her at any time, but they chose to wait until just two weeks before the coronation. Why that particular day?"

"We're back to the letters. There could be something in them—something about Princess Stella—that made someone decide to kidnap Alice."

"Then I guess someone could be trying to stop the coronation," Xena said. "Miss Jenny and her husband have a reason for *not* wanting Alice to be crowned. If we're right about the switched babies, it's Miss Jenny, and not Alice, who should be the next queen!"

"So if the letters say something about the

queen or Sherlock thinking that the baby who was returned wasn't really the princess, Miss Jenny and her family wouldn't have any motive for stealing the letters. Just the opposite—they'd want to tell everybody what's in them."

"That's a big *if*," Xena said.

"I know," Xander conceded. "But do you have another theory?"

Xena screwed up her face in thought. "No," she admitted. "Let's explore it a bit more." They sat in silence for what seemed like a long time.

"Okay," Xena finally said slowly. "What if we have it backward? What if someone isn't trying to *stop* the coronation—what if they're trying to hurry it up?"

"Why would they want to do that?"

"Maybe someone wants the coronation to happen *before* Alice gets a chance to find out she's not the real princess. That way she'd be crowned before she could change her mind about the Rathonian thing. Remember, she said she was for it but she didn't sound too sure."

"But what if—" Xander stopped. "Xena, can they have a secret coronation?"

"A secret coronation?"

"You know, like when that friend of Mom's

got married—they had a small wedding, just the two of them, because her husband was going into the army, and then when he came back, they had a big wedding with a cake and everything. But they were still married, even before the fancy wedding. Can they do that with a coronation?"

"I hope not." Suddenly, Xena felt sick to her stomach. "I just remembered something."

"What?"

"It was when we were looking up things about Borogovia—remember? There was a story about Alice's grandfather. He was sick in a hospital in Switzerland when his own father died. World War Two was just breaking out, and he had to be crowned in a hurry. The prime minister went to Switzerland with the crown, and they had the coronation there in the hospital."

She didn't need to tell Xander why this was so worrisome. They had been assuming that Alice would have to be taken to Borogovia for her coronation. If she could be crowned anywhere once she turned thirteen, then they had only four days until her birthday, and no idea of how to find her.

"Why didn't you tell me this before?" Xander demanded.

"I didn't think it was important. But there's a bright side—we're lucky there was that transportation strike!" Xena said. "All the airports and harbors in England and Scotland were closed when Alice disappeared. They didn't even let in private boats or planes. The trains and buses weren't even running and they searched all the cars and trucks leaving the country. So she couldn't have been taken out of the country while it was going on. And now that everyone knows she's missing, it's too late for the kidnapper to sneak her out after the strike ends. Her disappearance is all over the news, and the airports and seaports and bus stations are being watched. Nobody can sneak her out now."

"But if whoever kidnapped her has a secret coronation, it won't matter if they can't get her out," Xander said, his heart sinking. "The Borogovian constitution says that once you're crowned in the special ceremony, you're the ruler no matter what. Even if we could prove that she's not descended from Queen Charlotte and King Boris, she'd be the queen. And there's nothing anyone can do about it."

CHAPTER THIRTEEN

The next morning, Xander woke early and couldn't get back to sleep. He got up and wandered into the kitchen. Another gloomy day, he noticed as he saw the low gray clouds. It was Wednesday, halfway through spring break, and he didn't feel any closer to a solution to Alice's disappearance.

He could tell from the cereal bowl in the sink that Xena was already up too. She never remembered to put her dirty dishes in the dishwasher. He had his own breakfast and then went into the study, where he found his sister tapping on the computer keyboard.

"Look at this," she said.

He came around and read over her shoulder, and then straightened. "If it's true what they say here—that babies' fingerprints don't last as long as grown-ups'—no wonder Sherlock couldn't use them to identify the princess, or whoever the new baby was. It wasn't his fault."

"Still, at least he was using cutting-edge technology to solve his crime, just like we do!" Xena couldn't help being cheered by this thought.

"You two are up early for a vacation day," their mother said as she came in and turned on a light. "This case must be keeping you busy."

"It is," Xander said.

"Well, here's something that should make it easier," their mother said as she poured herself a cup of coffee. "The transit strike ended last night. So now you won't have to be dependent on me or your dad or that nice Mr. Brown to get around for your investigations."

"I guess," Xena said.

Mrs. Holmes paused on her way out the door. "Oh, Xena, I've been meaning to ask. What do you think of that new cell phone?"

Xena and Xander exchanged glances. "It's okay. Nothing special." She hadn't yet dared tell her mother that the phone had gone missing along with Alice.

"I forgot to activate the GPS feature," her mother said. "I think I need to program something to make it work."

"What GPS feature?" Xander asked. Suddenly, they were both alert.

"It's a way for parents to keep track of where their children are. I thought you knew. You can track where the phone is once the feature is activated. I'm not sure how to do it, so after you get home, let me have it so that I can figure it out, okay?" She left the room.

"I sure hope she isn't going to spy on me," Xena said, but Xander wasn't listening.

"Maybe we can use the GPS to figure out where Alice is!" He ran out of the room and came back a moment later with a booklet. "I told Mom I wanted to try to activate it myself, so she gave me the instructions. They're not online yet because the phone is kind of secret."

"She said she had to have the phone to activate the GPS," Xena pointed out. "We don't have the phone, and anyway, it's turned off. It's no good, Xander."

"Don't give up so easily!" Xander was already on his own cell phone. "Hello, Andrew? Oh, sorry. I didn't realize it was so early. Listen, though, this is important, and we need someone techie like you." He grinned at Xena, who knew as well as he did how well flattery worked with

Andrew. Xander explained the situation and said, "Okay, call me back."

"Andrew's going to look it up," Xander said after he'd hung up. "He said that even though this phone is new and experimental, it sounds familiar. It might be the second generation of another phone, one where the specs *are* online. That one can be programmed remotely, so maybe this one can too."

"When he calls back, put him on speaker." Xena still didn't think that the phone would help them find Alice, but she didn't know what else to do.

Xander's phone buzzed. "Hi, Andrew. I'm putting you on speaker."

"I found it!" Andrew sounded excited, which was rare. "Give me the serial number and everything else you have." Xena read from the booklet, and Andrew said, "If this new phone is like the first generation, it has a secondary backup battery that can't be turned off. Hold on a sec." They waited. "Okay, I think I activated the GPS. It's finding the phone."

Xena couldn't remain in her seat. She stood behind Xander and held her breath.

Andrew read an address. Xena was about

to write it down when Xander said, "Are you kidding?"

"That's what it says." Andrew repeated the address. "Why, what's the matter?"

"Not sure," Xander said. "We'll get back to you. Thanks, Andrew."

"What *is* it, Xander? You've got to tell me!" Xena couldn't stand the suspense.

"The address that Andrew gave me is the Borogovian mansion."

Xena felt suddenly deflated. "So that means Alice left it behind when she was kidnapped, after all."

"Wait a second," Xander said slowly. "Something's been bothering me. It seems like an awfully big coincidence for the security cameras to be knocked out by the thunderstorm just at the moment Alice 'ran away,' don't you think?"

"Maybe the kidnappers turned off the cameras *before* the storm, and they were just lucky that a storm came up to give them an alibi. If there hadn't been a storm, they would have had to come up with some other reason the cameras were turned off—maintenance or an accident or something," Xena said.

"Or maybe they planned the kidnapping for

a night when a storm was predicted," Xander suggested.

"It's also possible that someone in the security team was in on the kidnapping and blocked the cameras somehow," Xena added. "There are lots of explanations."

"And there's one more," Xander said. *"Maybe Alice never left."*

They stood frozen in thought, trying to figure out what that meant, and if it was true, how the police could have missed her.

"When you have eliminated the impossible—" Xander reminded Xena, starting one of their ancestor's most famous sayings.

"—whatever remains, however improbable, must be the truth," she finished for him. It was not exactly impossible that the security system had been accidentally disabled at just the moment when Alice left—or was taken from the mansion—but the odds against it were astronomical.

Xander's phone beeped, signaling a text message. Probably Andrew. But no, the phone showed that the message came from Xena's phone. Xena leaned over Xander's shoulder and together they read: "Hello, Xena! Sorry I wasn't here when you came looking for me. I had to go away for a little while, but everything's just fine. Don't bother trying to find me! Sincerely, Alice."

"Yeah, right," Xander said with contempt.

"There's no way Alice wrote that." Xena nearly laughed. "Nobody would write a text with capital letters and punctuation. And 'Sincerely, Alice.' Oh, sure! Someone else wrote it, someone who has no idea how to text. There must have been a signal on my phone that showed we'd turned on the GPS, and whoever has Alice saw it and got nervous, and sent us this to get us off the trail."

"As if!" Xander said.

They were both immensely cheered by the knowledge that they were getting close enough to frighten the kidnapper, though Xena tried not to think how dangerous this might be for Alice. The sooner they found her, the better.

"Let me have your phone," she said to Xander. She punched in Andrew's number. "Hello, Andrew? Can you tell where my phone was when the earlier message was sent—the one that really looks like Alice wrote it, the one we showed to the police?"

"When was that?"

146

She told him. She heard computer keys clicking, and then Andrew said, "That one came from the same address."

"Thanks." Xena shut the phone. "So that means Alice is still in the mansion—or at least she was when the first message was sent. But where could she be? And who put her there?"

"We haven't really thought about the prime minister," Xander said.

"No good." Xena shook her head. "He wasn't even in London when Alice was kidnapped." She stopped at the knowing smile on her brother's face. "Or maybe he was! We have only his word for it that he arrived after she disappeared."

"Let's find out when he checked into his hotel," Xander suggested.

"We don't know what hotel he's staying in," Xena said.

"We can figure it out. Remember he said there was construction outside? Let's find out which hotels are near construction sites."

In a short time, Xena had identified all of London's best hotels, ones that looked like places an important foreigner would stay. Then she found a traffic site that warned of construction in the city. It was easy to put the two together and figure out that the prime minister was most likely staying at the Hotel Bertrand. Two different Tube lines ran near it, so it should be easy to get to, she thought.

They set out for the Tube station in silence, Xena holding an umbrella over both of them. As they stopped and waited for a light to change, Xander's eye caught a figure standing under a lamppost. Why would someone just stand there in the rain? If he—or she—was waiting for someone, why didn't he go into a store or at least stand under an awning? "Xena, look over there," he said in a low voice and jerked his head the slightest bit toward the unmoving person.

Xena pretended the wind had caught her umbrella, and she glanced at it and behind her shoulder as she pulled it closer overhead. She instantly saw the person Xander was referring to, wrapped in a dark raincoat with a hood pulled down tight, casting a shadow on the face. She couldn't tell if it was a man or a woman. Although the person appeared to be staring at nothing, Xena could tell that he—or she—was really keeping an eye on her and her brother.

Hardly moving her lips, Xena said, "We'll have to separate. I'll try to get him to follow me, and then I'll lose him. Meet me at that church, Saint Bartholomew the Great, in twenty minutes. If I'm not there, call Mom and tell her what happened. If we shake him, we can go to the hotel, each of us on a different Tube line just in case."

Xander nodded, and the instant the light changed, he sprinted across the street and dodged pedestrians. Although he wasn't as fast a runner as Xena, he was a good soccer player who was used to weaving around opponents, and he soon disappeared.

Just as Xena had hoped, their follower hesitated when the two of them split up. Xena took a moment to close her umbrella and then ran around the corner, hoping the stranger would follow her. It was hard to tell in the rain, but it did sound like running footsteps were behind her. She didn't stop to look around until the road curved, and then she was able to see that although the person was still there, the distance between them was increasing with every stride of her well-trained legs.

Around another corner, through an alley, and then over a small brick wall, and Xena was sure she had shaken her pursuer. She took a roundabout route to the old church, which had a tiny open square in front of it. She pushed open the heavy door and entered the gloom.

"What took you so long?" Xander stepped out from behind a gray stone column. "I was just about to call Mom!"

Xena shook her head without answering, as she was working hard to get her breath back. She gestured toward the back of the church, where she remembered there was a door leading to a small garden. Few churches had exits in that part of the building, so if, despite all her efforts, she had been followed, the person would probably assume they were still inside and wouldn't be able to leave except through the front door. Their pursuer would be waiting there, ready to pounce.

They took separate Tube lines and met up, as planned, in the park in front of the Hotel Bertrand. They had seen the hotel from a distance—it was close to the British Museum— but now they stood and stared before going in, not minding the rain that fell on their faces as they looked up. It was huge and ornate, built of reddish brown stone, with lots of windows, balconies, complicated architecture, doors, stairways, and other details that were almost overwhelming.

The lobby was small but gleaming with marble, and the clerks behind the desk looked as though they had been polished. A young Asian woman smiled at them as they came in.

Xander turned on all his charm, but the clerk wouldn't budge. "We can't give out our guests' room numbers or any information on their stay with us. If you like, I can call the party you're here to visit, and he can give us permission to send you up." She poised her hand over the house phone.

"Thank you," Xena said hastily. "But we want it to be a surprise. We'll figure out something."

They went back outside and stood on the sidewalk, discouraged.

"I thought there was supposed to be construction going on around here," Xander said, surveying the cars moving by, unimpeded by anything except the traffic lights.

A voice behind them said, "They do it only at night, so as not to mess up traffic too badly." They turned, and the hotel doorman said, "Why, it's the Holmes kids!"

It was their old friend, a member of the SPFD who had worked as the doorman at the hotel where they stayed when they first moved to London. They chatted for a few minutes, and found out that he now worked at the Hotel Bertrand.

"So what are you two doing here? Working on a case?"

"We were hoping to speak with the prime minister from Borogovia," Xander told him. "The princess who disappeared is a friend of ours."

The doorman shook his head. "The prime minister isn't here. You just missed him. He came back for a nap and went out again only a few minutes ago. Last night, he reported another attempted burglary in his room. Security didn't find anything, but it disturbed his sleep. The construction is annoying him too. The front desk warned him about it when he checked in, but evidently he didn't realize how serious it was. Look at how much work they're doing!"

He gestured to a drawing on the chain-link fence over a hole in the ground. The architect's rendition showed a complex mass of lines and squiggles. Xander stared at it, and Xena asked,

"Couldn't he tell for himself how much work they were doing?"

"No, I told you, the construction only goes on at night. The prime minister was here hours before it started, and then the rain delayed it even more. They didn't get going until the wee, small hours."

Xander objected, "But he checked in—" He was about to blurt out "at night" when Xena dug her elbow in his ribs. She didn't want their friend to get in trouble for revealing so much about a guest. They hurriedly said good-bye, promised to send his regards to their parents, and withdrew into the park across the street for a quick consultation.

"So the prime minister arrived in the afternoon, not at night! He *was* here when Alice disappeared. Why would he lie about—" Xena stopped. Xander had that absorbed look on his face again, so she waited.

She didn't have to wait long. "Something's been bugging me ever since we saw those papers from the SPFD," he said. "I couldn't figure out what it was, but I think it was something about the blueprints for the addition to the Borogovian mansion. I didn't read all of them, and they were pretty complicated. Let's go back to the SPFD and look at them."

It took them only a few minutes on the Tube. Even that seemed long, and they ran up the escalator to the street, saying "Excuse me, excuse me" as they brushed past commuters and tourists. They slowed down as they entered the pub, not wanting to draw attention to themselves, then crawled through the hidden door and burst into the SPFD headquarters.

"No time to explain," Xander said to Mr. Brown. "Can we see those Borogovian papers again?"

Mr. Brown pointed at the box, still sitting on the table. Xander pulled out paper after paper and lined up the blueprints, one next to the other. "What are you—" Mr. Brown started, but Xena put her finger on her lips.

What seemed like a long time went by while Xander moved the papers around. He put one drawing over another and held them up to the light, measuring things with his thumb. Finally, he looked up and beamed. "Got it!"

CHAPTER FOURTEEN

Got it? Got *what*?" Xena felt ready to explode.

"Look at this." Xander put a finger of his right hand on one blueprint and a finger of his left hand on another one.

Xena looked. "I don't see it. What exactly are you trying to show me?"

"There's a space that's unaccounted for in these drawings that the architects made, the ones who built this addition for Queen Charlotte. See? This wall"—he pointed to a solid line at the left-hand edge of one piece of paper— "is supposed to be the same wall as this one." He ran his finger along the right-hand side of another sheet. "But if you add up the measurements of how long all the walls are, they're not the same. There's a gap, about ten feet. It could be nothing—a mistake in the drawings, an error where the architects left a blank space, even something to support the addition, but I don't think so. I think it's a—"

"A hidden room!" Xena finished for him.

Mr. Brown didn't wait for an explanation. In a flash he was on the phone, calling the police. "Meet us at the Borogovian mansion. I'll explain once we're there. And be sure to come with a search warrant." He turned to Xena and Xander. "Out you go. My car is around the corner."

They had just fastened their seat belts when Mr. Brown punched a button on his dashboard and a siren started wailing. "There's a light flashing on the roof too," he said.

Traffic parted in front of them as they sped through the streets and pulled up in front of the Borogovian mansion. They leaped out onto the sidewalk, where four police officers were waiting for them. One was the man who had ignored the evidence of the handwriting and the text message, and he was as red as the light flashing on Mr. Brown's car. Another man, evidently his superior, was saying in an incredulous tone, "And on your own authority, you ignored it? Don't you know who these kids are? If they say they have information, you can wager that they do! You're relieved of duty as soon as we finish up here, pending an investigation into your actions." Xena knew she should feel sorry for the man, but she couldn't help feeling a bit smug too.

They stood in front of the big iron gate, and once again a cold voice demanded to know who they were. "Metropolitan Police," barked the police officer who appeared to be in charge. "I'm Inspector Sayers." He held the search warrant up to the camera, and the gate swung open.

"This way!" Xander ran ahead of the police. A servant opened the door and stood back as first Xander, then Xena, and then the police and Mr. Brown ran in.

They tore down one corridor after another. Xena, as always, marveled that Xander remembered exactly which way to go.

Xander threw open a door and revealed Alice's aunt Penelope with the Borogovian prime minister sitting in front of a fireplace. Both stood up, Aunt Penelope with her hand to her throat.

"What is the meaning of this intrusion?" she demanded, addressing the adults as though Xena and Xander were of no consequence.

Xena stepped forward. "We think you kidnapped Alice. We also think that she's somewhere here, in this mansion."

"Why on earth would I kidnap my own niece? It wouldn't even be kidnapping; I'm her legal guardian and she's underage!"

"There's such a thing as false imprisonment," the inspector said grimly. "We are going to search the premises again." He dispatched the three officers in different directions. Occasionally Xena and Xander heard a deep voice calling, "Princess Alice! Your Highness! It's the police!"

Xander approached the prime minister. "I'd like to ask you a few questions, sir."

"Of course, of course. Anything that we can do. Although I don't know any more than you do. I arrived in London after Her Highness had disappeared."

"Er—" Xena didn't want to tell him to his face that he was lying, but she knew he was. She looked at Xander.

"Sir," he began, "are you sure of when you arrived? Because"—he had to speak hastily before the prime minister could get a word in—"because someone told us that you got in a little earlier than that."

"Who told you that?" the inspector asked.

"A friend," Xena said, hoping he wouldn't

ask any more than that. Luckily, the prime minister answered.

"Your friend is right." The prime minister sat down heavily. He took a large handkerchief from his pocket and wiped his face with it. "I did get in earlier on Saturday, but I had nothing to do with Princess Alice's disappearance. Please believe me."

"How do we know that?" Inspector Sayers asked.

The prime minister pulled a wad of paper out of another pocket. "Here are receipts for the restaurants I went to that night. I adore English food, and I knew that once I became caught up in preparations for the coronation, I would be too busy to indulge this passion. The steak and kidney pie! Bubble and squeak!"

"Muffins!" Xander couldn't help adding. Xena glowered at him.

"If you check the time stamped on the receipts," the prime minister went on, "I think you'll see that I couldn't have been involved in this ghastly occurrence."

One by one, the three policemen returned. Before they even spoke, their disappointed faces revealed that their search had been unsuccessful.

"Nothing, sir," one of them told Mr. Brown.

"Exactly as I said!" Aunt Penelope trumpeted.

Inspector Sayers began, "I'm afraid—"

"May I take a look?" Xander interrupted him.

The inspector glanced at Mr. Brown. He nodded. The prime minister said, "Of course you may. No harm in it, is there?" he asked Aunt Penelope, who pinched her lips together for a moment and then nodded ungraciously.

Xena followed her brother up the stairs. He didn't need to tell her what he was doing. Obviously, he was looking for the place where he had found the mysterious gap in the architectural drawings. Close behind her came the inspector and Mr. Brown. She remembered that Alice's interrupted text message mentioned being taken "up." But up where?

Xander didn't stop at the second floor but kept on until he was at the landing between the second and third floors. The wall was covered by a large scene of the countryside, with picturesque shepherdesses, birds, flowers, a small hut. It was one of those *trompe l'œil* paintings, like the ones Miss Jenny had shown them on their first visit, and in the dim light of the stairway,

Xena could have sworn that she was really looking at a sunny afternoon in the country.

Xander ran his hands over the painting. Alice's aunt Penelope shouted, "Stop! You'll dirty it!" Xander ignored her and worked his fingers around a crack.

The "hut" was really a door in the wall! Xander knocked on it and shouted, "Alice! Alice! Are you in there?" Xena thought she heard a faint voice.

Mr. Brown stepped up. "Will you show us how to open this, madam, or will we have to break it down?"

"I have no idea what you're talking about!" Aunt Penelope said, so a large policeman slammed his shoulder into the door three times. It burst open.

CHAPTER FIFTEEN

Standing on a chair under a skylight was Alice.

Gemma wriggled through the crowd of policemen and ran to her friend. Alice jumped down from the chair, and the two girls hugged for a long time.

Miss Jenny hurried in. "Are you all right?" she asked Alice, who nodded and then burst into tears. Miss Jenny led the two girls out into the corridor. The police crowded around them until Miss Jenny said, "Leave her alone! First let me get a cup of tea into her, and then you can ask all the questions you want."

"It's all right," Alice said, with more firmness than Xena and Xander had ever heard from her. "I want to tell you now."

Xander saw that the police inspector had quietly moved down a step or two and was standing below both Jasper and Alice's aunt, blocking their exit.

"What were you doing on that chair?" Gemma asked.

"Trying to get out." Alice turned to her aunt. "I didn't believe you when you said you were hiding me for my own safety. I knew that could not be true. But what did you want?" she demanded. "You told me that you had to hide me because there was a threat on my life and we had to hurry the coronation before anyone found out where I was. But I *knew* you were lying!"

"Is that why you sent me that text?" Xander asked.

Alice's eyes were still blazing, and she made an obvious effort to control herself. "Yes. I heard them coming and pressed SEND before I could finish, and he"—pointing at Jasper—"took the phone."

"I was looking out for your best interests," her aunt said. "I knew that you were being exposed to all sorts of influences." She looked pointedly at Miss Jenny, who glared back at her. "I was going to take you to Borogovia last Saturday evening, so that you could prepare for the coronation in peace, without silly people trying to convince you that Borogovia would be better off independent."

"But you didn't know there would be a transit strike!" Xander said. "Then you were stuck! Even when the strike ended, you couldn't get out of the country because by then word had gotten out that Alice was missing."

"So you panicked." Xena picked up the tale. "You were in a hurry to get her away from us before she could figure out what those letters meant."

"Letters?" The police inspector looked baffled, but Aunt Penelope's expression told Xena that she was on the right track, and she pressed on before the woman could regain her composure.

"The only thing you could think of was to say she had run away, so you wrote that note supposedly from her."

"What note?" Alice asked. "I didn't write a note! How *could* you, Aunt Penelope?"

"And then," Xander went on, "you were going to crown her here and try to convince her to support Rathonia taking over poor little Borogovia!"

"How did you plan to crown her?" the prime

minister asked, "given that I'm the one who always carries the crown?"

"The break-ins at the hotel!" Xena and Xander exclaimed together.

Xander caught a movement out of the corner of his eye. "It's Jasper—he's getting away!"

The bodyguard had taken advantage of the inspector's distraction to slip past him and was now running down the stairs. He was dangerously fast, and all the officers were crowded around the room where Alice had been hidden. They bumped into one another trying to get down the stairs, each slowing the others down. Jasper was getting away!

Xena vaulted over the banister and landed on the second floor, where the stairs turned. She crouched right in Jasper's path, and before he could stop, he tripped over her and went sprawling at full length. He sprang up, but not quickly enough. The policeman who had ignored Xena and Xander's clues tackled him and held him still while one of his colleagues handcuffed him and hauled him to his feet.

"It's not my fault!" The bodyguard narrowed his eyes and pointed an accusing finger at Alice's aunt. "She's the one who thought of it!"

"You tried to steal the crown from the prime minister, didn't you? And you stole the birth certificate?" Xena asked. The shame on Jasper's face gave away his guilt.

"I don't believe that you were acting purely out of obedience to orders," the prime minister said. "Come on, tell us the rest."

"She said"—once again indicating Aunt Penelope—"that when she got paid by the Rathonian government, she would reward me."

"You were in the pay of Rathonia?" Gemma was on her feet. "Why, you're a traitor!"

"Arrest them!" the prime minister said.

"There's more!" Xander said. Quickly, he and Xena explained what they found in the archives, and that they suspected that in Sherlock's time Princess Stella had been swapped with the nanny's daughter, Josephine Blunt.

Alice's mouth dropped open. She snapped it shut. "That's what those letters must have been about," she said.

The prime minister looked as though he couldn't take in one more fact, but he asked faintly, "Letters? What letters?"

Alice explained. The silence that followed was broken by her aunt.

"She's imagining that!" Aunt Penelope snapped. "The girl lives in a fantasy world! She did find some old papers, that's true, but they had nothing to do with her. Mere scribblings. I took them away and burned them. They were old and moldy, and I didn't want them to make her sick."

"You burned them?" The prime minister was aghast. "Documents from our nation's history?"

"Enough of this," Aunt Penelope said. "I'm still the girl's guardian, and she is the daughter of the king and queen of Borogovia. Nobody will believe that nonsense about another baby being substituted for Princess Stella, or that I was in the pay of a foreign government. Now that travel is possible, we will immediately go to Borogovia, where Alice will be crowned and she will take up her duties under my direction."

Xander's phone buzzed. He answered it and listened for a moment, then asked, "Can I put you on speaker?" He pressed some buttons and said, "It's Andrew Watson from the Society for the Preservation of Famous Detectives. He has results of a DNA test on Alice and Gemma."

Miss Jenny shot her daughter a puzzled look. Gemma looked clueless, but something serious in Xander's voice made everyone fall silent. He held up his phone so that they all could hear.

"The results are only preliminary," Andrew said. "They'll have to be confirmed by a lengthier process, but there doesn't appear to be much doubt."

"What did they find out?" Xander asked. "Come *on*, Andrew!"

"Independent laboratory results show that Subject B, not Subject A, is a member of the royal family of Borogovia."

"Who's Subject A?" Xena asked.

"Alice Banders." There was a gasp from Alice's aunt, and she started to say something, but the prime minister glared at her and she shut her mouth.

"And Subject B is . . . ?" Xander asked.

"Subject B is identified as Gemma Giles."

"Wait a second!" Miss Jenny said. "Does this mean—" She looked from Gemma to Alice and back again.

Gemma finished it for her. "It means that *you're* the heir to the throne of Borogovia, not Alice! And *I'm* the princess!"

A policeman holding handcuffs approached Aunt Penelope.

"Oh, please don't," Alice begged. "Can't you just let her go?"

"Sorry," Mr. Brown said as the police inspector led Penelope out. "What she did was a serious crime, and she has to be punished."

CHAPTER SIXTEEN

"Finally!" Xander nearly danced with impatience as his mother came in with a box from the bakery. "It's about to start!"

It was just over a week since Alice had been discovered in the hidden room in the Borogovian mansion. The definitive DNA test had come back, and there was no doubt that Miss Jenny and Gemma, not Alice, had the blood of the royal family of Borogovia in their veins.

The producers of *Talented Brits* knew that if someone who had been in the news so much sang on their program, the number of viewers would be enormous no matter how good or bad a singer she was, so they told Alice she didn't have to do the live audition. Now, the show was going to start in five minutes, and Xena and Xander were torn—see their friend sing on live

TV or watch Miss Jenny being crowned in the Borogovian capital?

"Scoot over," their mother said. Their father joined them on the couch, and they were so crowded they could hardly breathe. But nobody minded.

A troupe of jugglers took the stage on *Talented Brits*, so Xena clicked the remote. Pre-coronation ceremonies were being shown on the international channel. "Oh, I forgot to tell you," she said. "Miss Jenny called while you were out."

"Really?" Their mother sounded pleased. "About to be crowned, and she makes a phone call? She's a calm one!"

"Very," Xander said. "She'll be a good queen. What did she want?"

"She said that Alice's aunt confessed that she always suspected she and Alice weren't related to the royal family of Borogovia, and the letters confirmed her fears. She had to have the crown to make the coronation legal, but when Jasper failed to get it, she was going to go ahead with it anyway and hope that the Borogovian people would accept the coronation."

"Well, that clinches it." Xena clicked the remote again. "Oh, look!" Alice was taking the stage. She looked small in the spotlight until she began to sing. When she reached the end of the Borogovian national anthem, the crowd was on its feet. Alice, her cheeks pink and her eyes shining, took bow after bow.

"Quick! Let's look at the coronation!"

Miss Jenny, a gleaming crown on her head, was addressing a crowd in a huge, sparkling hall. She was speaking Borogovian, but Xena and Xander didn't need to read the subtitles. They knew that she was making a passionate speech about Borogovian independence.

Xander, his mouth full of muffin, glanced at Xena. Silently, she high-fived him. They had not only solved a case, but had also helped a friend and ensured that a tough little country would stand on its own feet.

School had started again on Monday, and Alice hadn't been there to sing the solo in the school concert. Xena and Xander Holmes didn't mind, though. It had been a great spring break!